The Pandora Machine

(The ABACUS Protocol #2)

Thea Gregory

www.PlanetThea.com

Chapter One

The world spun around the confines of Vivian's dormant mind, a mechanical humming boring into her ears. Or, were they alarm klaxons? She squirmed, stretching frozen muscles and ungluing her tongue from the roof of her mouth. Heaviness had settled itself into her limbs, and the red burning of a bright light overhead glowed through her eyelids. Had they left the Extra-Galactic Observatory yet? Did the rescue crews fix the problem?

She began to drift back to the near-death of stasis sleep. Then, a spike of pain shot through her arm and restraints twisted against her arms and legs, snaring her into place. She struggled, trying in vain to pull her arms towards herself.

"The patient is waking up, Doctor Powell," announced a measured and feminine synthetic voice. Vivian flinched as gloved fingers grazed her forearm.

"Thank you, Larissa, please notify the Council and make the arrangements to have her moved as soon as we've concluded here," replied a woman, whose voice was dry and held the edge of age and fatigue.

Vivian tried to force open her eyes. Parts of her last moments on the Extra-Galactic Observatory fluttered through her mind. She didn't know why she was restrained in a hospital—their departure had seemed normal, until the alarm sounded.

"Don't move too much, sweetie," the doctor said. "It won't help, and if I decide to sedate you, it will put you back under for another month." The machine jabbing into Vivian's arm was removed, leaving a throbbing pain that crawled up and down her limb. She lay still as instructed, but her mind was jumbled and grasping at probabilities and theories.

"Doctor, I will remind you that sedating her would be a violation of the Hippocratic Oath," interjected the computer.

"Don't you tell me about the Hippocratic Oath,

Larissa," Doctor Powell spat. Vivian felt cold droplets settle on her skin. "Now, send the revised readings and do your job."

A breeze wafted over Vivian, and the door slammed. She tested the restraints, but they held fast.

"The heaviness will pass in time, Vivian. You will be all right. Please do not be alarmed." Larissa said, breaking the silence that formed after Doctor Powell had stormed out of the room. "But, don't push too hard. A stasis pod malfunction is a serious medical emergency that requires careful observation and treatment."

Vivian tested the bonds again, only half-understanding what the computer said. Her voice was much like quIRK's, but different. She expected to hear his calm, impassive voice at any moment, announcing wake-up time or paging her to lunch. Would there be chocolate pie? she wondered, before snapping back into reality as though her consciousness were an elastic band wound backwards in time.

She took one deep breath, and then another. The air was thin and dry, laced with the scents of sterilization solutions and the byproducts of nanorobotic cleaning machines—devices found even in Aurora's subterranean hospitals. Microbes transformed from dangerous pathogens into harmless floral-scented molecules. The throbbing in her arm persisted, sending tingles down her fingers. She willed them to wiggle, and they obeyed, the motion jerky and hesitant. Thoughts and memories became ordered and rational, and the initial panic of the doctor's words faded into the heaviness that still laced her limbs and mind.

"Take it slow, Vivian. You're doing well," Larissa intoned. "Breathe as deeply as you can, and focus on the memories you have from before you went into the pod. They will center you, and help you overcome stasis sickness." Vivian had never encountered a supercomputer nurse before, but she was more inclined to trust it than a human. Programmed ethics couldn't be broken, or even easily bent. Something was amiss with the way she was being treated, especially the restraints, but her tongue remained a useless slab of meat no matter how hard she tried to will herself to speak. Questions burned in the back of her mind, but the words could not come.

Vivian pulled the memories back into her mind. The alarm. The soulless metal interior of the rescue ship. Alec's toothy smile. quIRK saying goodbye. But, quIRK wasn't gone, she had him, or at least a miniaturization of his mental processes tucked away in her bag. Her heart raced. What if they'd discovered him? She was done for if they found him, tucked away in a wooden flute case. The second sentient computer known to man, hiding away in her luggage. Had the stasis accident affected him, as well? She focused on that final moment before going to sleep—she had to remember if he was packed in a stasis chamber, or normal storage. She hoped it was the latter; a stasis malfunction severe enough to put her in the hospital would have likely destroyed the delicate patchwork of circuitry she had created for him.

"Slow your breathing, Vivian. You're going to hyperventilate," Larissa said, interrupting Vivian's thoughts. "Stay calm, don't worry about your current situation. You need to be healthy before we can do anything." She's better at this than quIRK ever was, Vivian thought, with a twinge of guilt. quIRK had been her friend, however eccentric he had been. She hoped that he'd managed to evade the audit team. She remembered them now, too, along with her friends. Alec the goofball. Robert the scientist, even the cats—Lepton and Muon.The diabolical Bryce Zimmer.

Vivian pried her eyes open, and was immediately blinded by the lights in the ceiling. She clamped her eyes shut, spots dancing across her field of vision.

"I will dim the lights. You are doing very well, Vivian. Look around the room, and remember to breathe slowly and deeply as you acclimate," Larissa said. Compared to quIRK's impassive monotone, she gave the illusion of being sentient, though Vivian doubted that was the case.

Vivian coaxed her eyes open again, and let them wander around the small, darkened room. Her vision was blurry despite the adaptive eye lenses she'd had fitted as a child, and she blinked, hard, several times in an attempt to clear the fuzziness. She could make out a holographic display dominating the far wall, its mix of colors and shapes shining brightly like a holo-billboard she'd seen in passing on the Epsilon Eridani hub, months ago. Could it have been a year ago? Many years? Turning her attention to herself, Vivian saw that she was lying under a thin hospital blanket, and her arms and feet were secured to the railing of the bed by leathery plastic restraints. They were as strong as steel, but would cause little damage to the limbs if she were to struggle. A machine sat to the right of her aching arm—it had many wires, each attached to an electrode or a needle. She shuddered and looked away.

The rest of the room was empty. A lonely white bench sat next to the door, across from a wide window. Outside the window lay a vast city of low-rise white buildings interspersed with trees and crisscrossed by translucent aerial tubes the round pods that could only be the orbital taxis she'd seen in vids. The sky was deep blue and laced with clouds. Vivian had never seen anything like it. The sea lay beyond city's coast line, stretching out into the horizon. A large moon hung just over the sea, its faint white surface pocked and scarred with craters. The vista was incredible, as mind-shattering as that first time she'd looked into the heart of the Milky Way galaxy. She wished she were outside, so she could stand under the yellow sun, and gaze up at a night sky unobscured by the auroras burning across the stars.

"Where?" she tried to speak. The word caught in her throat and her swollen tongue slurred the word almost beyond recognition.

"You're in the Earth Memorial New Damascus Superhospital," Larissa began. "We're located in the capital city of Jasmine. This is a secure wing that specializes in intensive care for patients who require special protective protocols to be in place. You are not a prisoner, but the New Damascus Science Authority believed it was prudent to limit access to you while you're in recovery."

So, she was on New Damascus, and apparently not in custody despite her restraints. But, who were they protecting her from? So many questions tumbled through her jumbled mind. What questions would Larissa answer? She had to have rules concerning information dissemination, and confidentiality. Maybe Bryce got away, she thought with a sudden shudder.

"Why am I here?" Vivian forced the words out, daring her mouth and throat to deny her. She'd been through enough, she wanted answers and an explanation so she could be on her way to the Ithaca colony's new observatory and her latest job.

"Your stasis pod experienced a mechanical malfunction and was set to deep space mode, a setting designed for sleep periods of over fifty years," Larissa paused, allowing Vivian an instant to process this new information. "As you spent only four months in stasis, the wake-up period was abrupt and dangerous. Had you not been close to a hospital, the neural stress and resultant cardiac arrest would have killed you. Fortunately, you were in excellent physical condition and were able to recover more quickly than expected; you only took six weeks to come out of the recuperative coma that followed all of your nanosurgeries."

Vivian gasped. It was impossible, the trip from the Extra-Galactic Observatory to New Damascus only took slightly over four weeks. "Four months?" she managed to ask.

"The rescue vessel's progress was delayed by an unforeseen event," came the reply.

"Event?" Vivian asked. Her tongue was loosening, but her throat was still raspy.

"That information is classified pending an investigation from the New Damascus Science Authority." Vivian was grateful for the effects of the stasis accident now—she could not have contained her shock and culpability otherwise. They must have found quIRK, she realized, and her heart fell into the hollow of her stomach.

"When do I go to Ithaca?" she asked, hoping that she could get as far away from that investigation as possible. The frontier would be the ideal place for her.

"You have been placed on indefinite leave pending the results of the investigation. You must remain on New Damascus as a witness and a person of interest who will, if necessary, appear before the tribunal, and also at the trial and inquest into the administration of Bryce Zimmer."

"How long will that take?" A tear trickled down her face, and she shuddered at the mention of Bryce, the man who'd tried to kill her multiple times. Only quIRK's intervention had saved her then, and it seemed that the megalomaniac was going to have another chance to ruin her.

"Don't cry, Vivian." Larissa's voice cut through the hollow place inside Vivian's stomach. "I am familiar with the station's incident reports, and he can't hurt you again. Not here. That's over, and there will always be work and assignments for a talented young woman like you. There is no date for the formal hearings to begin, and I recommend that you focus on getting well before becoming part of the investigation into Bryce Zimmer's administration."

Vivian only nodded, and took a shaky breath. This was not the future she'd had in mind for herself. At least Larissa had interpreted her body language as a form of post-traumatic stress, rather than the fear of her own crimes being exposed. Vivian believed that she'd done nothing wrong in helping quIRK escape the station and quIRK's demise, but she knew that the majority of humanity would condemn her for saving one artificial life.

All there was for her to do now was rest, and try to come to terms with the fact that over five months of her life had vanished in a stasis-induced coma. She'd never liked the idea of stasis, or the uncomfortable questions about the continuity of life that frequent stasis travel implied. But, to lose a third of a year was unfathomable.

It was something she was going to have to get used to, because for the moment her life was put on hold pending some bureaucratic tribunal. How could the deepest friendship she'd ever had be a crime?

Vivian hoped they would blame it all on Bryce.

Chapter Two

Vivian sat on the bench by the door, gazing out the window into the depths of the blue sky. She found that it was the sky, rather than the sea, that calmed her nerves. It had been about eight hours since she'd woken up, and only after a great deal of pleading did Larissa finally release her restraints and let her move to the bench. The door was still locked—Vivian couldn't leave the room—but the view would keep her entertained for the moment.

Vivian was still wearing a simple hospital gown, its beige tones blended with the off-peach walls of her room. The holo-display next to the window was a mess of readings, charts, and other medical information. She didn't have a clue what any of it meant, but she was comforted by the upward trend on all of her vital statistics.

"How am I doing, Larissa?" Vivian asked.

"You are doing very well, Vivian," the computer replied. "As I'm sure you've noticed, all of your readings are improving."

Vivian nodded. "Shouldn't I be weak? I did spend six weeks in a coma."

"We can medically prevent muscle atrophy, Vivian. It's very similar to stasis. Your good level of physical fitness helped you recover more quickly than the norm."

"Why don't I have any scars?"

"Nanorobots performed your surgeries. After injection, I directed their work remotely."

Vivian shuddered. "Machines, inside of me?" She rubbed her arms.

"Don't worry, Vivian. They were deactivated after use, and they decayed within a few hours."

Vivian looked down at her arms. "When can I leave, Larissa?" Even if her employment was on hold, she was eager to go somewhere, maybe visit Alec, wherever he was. Calypso Station, maybe.

"Doctor Powell will need to approve my recommendation after I have concluded my observation period."

"You're the one who makes the recommendations? How does that work?" Vivian was curious about how much autonomy they would allow a medical supercomputer.

"My qualifications and specifications would be of interest to you professionally as well as personally, if you would prefer that I elaborate."

"Please do," replied Vivian. She might not be quIRK, but Larissa could be a friend to her—as much of a friend as a non-sentient supercomputer could be.

"I am based on post-ABACUS technology, "Larissa said. Vivian's eyes were drawn to a flash on the holoscreen for an instant. "I feature the most advanced psychological programming, as well as having access to the most advanced medical equipment and knowledge in the galaxy. Built three years ago, I have comparable processing power to the deep-space quIRK units that you are familiar with, but with improved personality stability and bedside manner. In an emergency, I can replace a doctor. However, my recommendations are meant to supplement, rather than replace human judgment."

"So, you're based on quIRK?" Vivian had

suspected that she used similar programming, but she had no idea that a hospital would require the processing power of a deep-space telescope. It did make sense, if you assumed that the human body possessed a similar level of complexity to a galaxy or nebula.

"In a manner of speaking, I am an evolution of quIRK," Larissa replied. Vivian smirked at that. "I uphold the values of the Hippocratic Oath, and ensure the smooth functioning of the hospital, as well as anticipate threats to public health based on galactic trends and reports. Because of my increased stability, I do not require bi-yearly memory purges and many of the more draconian implementations of the ABACUS Protocol."

"But, do you like cats? What's your favorite color?" Vivian snickered at the thought of a cat-crazed hospital AI arguing about antiblue.

"Cats and other companion animals are an important part of the healing process. If you like, I can have one brought to your room now that you're awake. My favorite color is blue, like the sea. It is helpful to pick a color that humans can perceive. As pleasant as I find antired, starting arguments with patients is not my prerogative."

Vivian's eyes went wide. "You really are an evolution of quIRK. I think he picked fights with Alec on purpose!"

"Your friend, Alec Stone?"

"He's here? Is he okay?" Vivian bounded to her feet and grasped the door handle. It didn't budge, but she persisted.

"Alec was discharged on arrival and proceeded to Calypso, but only after being escorted to the orbital taxi by security," Larissa said. "He didn't want to leave you here, alone. A confrontational individual, but a very loyal friend to you." Despite being a disembodied voice, Larissa's words compelled Vivian to relax, and her grip on the door handle relaxed.

"Was he all right?"

"He was unharmed, but demanded that I personally inform him the moment you woke up. I sent the message six hours ago, but it is still early in the morning in the Epsilon Eridani system."

"Can I talk to—?" Vivian began, but she was cut off as the door opened. A tall, spindly older woman walked through, glaring down the bridge of her nose over a pair of brown-framed glasses. Her cold blue eyes locked on Vivian's, and Vivian resisted the urge to shudder. She wondered why a doctor wouldn't opt for adaptive vision correction treatments.

"It's about time you opened the door, Larissa. What were you talking about in here?" The woman's tone hadn't improved from earlier in the day.

"There appears to be a mechanical malfunction in the locking circuitry. This is a secure ward, all malfunctions result in lockdown." Vivian swallowed, hard. Mechanical malfunction was the word quIRK had used to obfuscate his sentience, and Bryce's sabotage.

"Why have you not contacted a custodian to repair it?" Doctor Powell asked Larissa

"All custodians are currently busy on higher

priority tasks."

"My patients always take priority from now on," the doctor growled. "While you're at it, do something about all those chain letters I keep getting. I hate cats!" Vivian sank down on the bench, and tried her best to become invisible.

"I will adjust the filters accordingly, Doctor Powell."

"That's what you said the last time, Larissa. This is the fourth one today." Doctor Powell walked over to the holo displays without so much as a nod towards Vivian, who fixed her eyes on the moon, which she had learned was named Antioch. She spoke again: "Good, you're recovering faster than expected. I will notify the Science Authority that their little media nightmare is awake. Maybe that will make the journalists leave me alone and you can be someone else's problem."

Doctor Powell stormed out of the room, leaving Vivian in a stunned silence. Why would the media care about her? Bryce was the administrator, and Alec had gone off to his next job.

"I apologize for Doctor Powell's outbursts. She is a competent doctor, but bedside manner is my specialty, not hers. I've observed that she resents the challenge I present to her authority."

"It's too bad you just can't take over," Vivian sighed.

"I value my life, and the last thing the galaxy needs is a third ABACUS Protocol violation. People are scared, and that's not a desirable element to introduce into a society."

"A third?" Vivian could not contain her surprise.

"The tabloids are rife with speculation on the full nature of the incident on the Extra-Galactic Observatory. The Science Authority's silence on the matter has only exasperated the situation. Hopefully, now that you're awake, they can clear the air and put people's minds at ease."

Vivian swallowed. "Is that why I'm a media nightmare?"

"You were moved to isolation to prevent exposure to external media before your debriefing.

They have been relentless in requesting updates on the murder witness who was hospitalized by a stasis accident. They seem eager to read conspiracy into mechanical errors."

"So I can't leave?" Vivian didn't want to be anywhere near this investigation. One wrong look, or a misplaced word and she was finished. Or, even worse, they could use advanced interrogation techniques to discern truth from lies.

"Not for the moment, but I'm sure that you'll be fine. It's a precaution to prevent widespread panic. This is only a temporary arrangement, to keep you from experiencing too much stress while you're recovering—after all, you did have most of your neurons re-polarized. I'll make sure nothing bad happens to you while you're here."

"Can I at least have access to my Gal-Net account? I want to tell my friends I'm okay, and it'll give me something to do for a while."

"I'll put in a request for an exception; hospital policy is that personal accounts are forbidden to patients in the secure wing. For now, I can put on a delayed-action news feed from local sources. There will be interruptions if something pertaining to the Extra-Galactic Observatory comes up, but it's better than nothing."

"Well, all right. What about my things?" Real-time broadcasts weren't popular on Aurora because of the persistent magnetic storms on its star, Helios, the cost of a view screen that was shielded from Helios' radiation was prohibitive to most families. She'd prefer to read one of her books, or play the flute.

"They're in secure storage and will be returned to you once all this is over," Larissa replied, as the window darkened and winked into a view screen, and the face of a female newscaster with a wide smile and curly black ringlets appeared on the screen. "Enjoy the programming, let me know if there is anything you need clarification on, or if you want to browse the other channels. I have the feed on a two-minute delay, which is standard."

"Thank you, Larissa." Vivian moved to the bed and curled up under the blankets. She forced her mind to focus on the newscaster's words, directing her energy into the day-to-day drama of a world that was not her own, and a city she would never call home.

Chapter Three

Vivian picked at a plate of hospital food, cringing at its mushy texture. Normally, she'd be overjoyed to try some of a new planet's local cuisine, but the presentation was simply unpalatable. She moved the food around her plate, and took small bites every time either hunger or Larissa prompted her to eat. Vivian couldn't imagine how the Extra-Galactic Observatory's mush-replicators had managed to prepare and serve better food than a planet-side hospital. She actually missed quIRK's wingfish pilaf, bluespargus, and chocolate pie. She was determined that her first meal outside the hospital would be in a cozy hub restaurant, while waiting for the shuttle to her next job.

Vivian had the video feed changed to galactic news about an hour ago, and despite the occasional blackout, there were few interruptions. She noted with some bitterness that the observatory that orbited the Ithaca colony was now operational. That should have been my job! she thought, cramming another fork full into her mouth.

The next story forced her to freeze in mid-chew:

"And in other news, New Damascus has offered to send a team of Informatics Specialists to the Epsilon Eridani hub, where a number of ships have been routed to improper destinations. Janus, the station's resident AI has been in operation for almost a century, and officials are claiming that these are isolated incidents related to the age of the computing equipment and the twenty percent increase in the number of hub links in the past three decades. Epsilon Eridani administrators say that no assistance is required, and add that travelers do not need to worry about delays or their own personal safety. Epsilon Eridani still falls under Earth jurisdiction, and thus they cannot be compelled to accept assistance from other systems." The voice went on into the details of the seven hundred year long history of the hub, but Vivian had ceased to listen. Larissa with her convenient door failure, and

Janus, the gatekeeper of the galaxy both experiencing issues may simply be a coincidence. But, after her own experience with quIRK, she didn't want to find herself at the mercy of any being —human or computer—ever again.

"Eat more, Vivian. You'll need your strength. An investigator is coming to visit you tomorrow morning." Larissa's voice broke through Vivian's melancholy, and jolted her back into reality.

"Then what? It's not like I have anywhere to go," Vivian said with a sigh.

"I have no additional information, but Doctor Powell will return to check your readings to ensure that you are healthy enough to go through with your meeting."

"It's not like I have much of a choice."

"No, but it's for the greater good. Your testimony will help revise safety standards and prevent similar incidents from happening on deep space assignments in the future. Think of your friend, Devon, and know that you can give his loved ones a sense of closure by telling the authorities what you know."

"That makes me feel better, thank you Larissa," Vivian lied, not at all reassured. Her stomach was tying itself in knots.

"I am attempting to contact your family, but intergalactic transmissions to Aurora are often slow and the authorities are difficult to work with because of the lag and solar storms. If they could provide arrangements, I could legally discharge you into their care for the duration of the investigation. I know you're not happy here, and I am working on a solution that keeps you safe, because it will take you a few more weeks to fully recover."

"Don't bother trying, they don't want me," Vivian looked down at her half-eaten food, focusing on the blue tint of her skin against the white plate.

"They're Traditionalists, then?" Larissa asked.

"And worse. Only my brother, Gareth, kept talking to me after dad kicked me out, but he stopped writing back years ago. I doubt they'd answer you at all—no offense, of course." Vivian choked on the words—she hadn't spoken her brother's name out loud in almost five years.

"I will keep trying. I am used to being rebuffed by humans. It is your nature to distrust what you don't understand."

"That's for sure, Larissa. Are you like this with all your patients?"

"I do my best to adapt to their needs, and listen to their fears and worries. Most just want to rant or despair and don't want my help, but I understand that illness is a vulnerable and frustrating time." Vivian was amazed by Larissa's level of self-awareness, and her ability to replicate the human notions of empathy and understanding. Even if it was just a sophisticated algorithm, was a computer's compassion any less real or valid than a human's?

"I'm glad you're helping me, Larissa," Vivian said. That, at least, was the truth.

"It is my function. I have received clearance for you to access a limited version of Gal-net. I will screen your outgoing and incoming messages." Vivian sat upright, grinning from ear to ear. Larissa continued: "First, I will require your retinal scan and hand print on the holographic terminal." As Larissa spoke, the holographic terminal mutated from its habitual medical charts and readings into the familiar Gal-net interface. Vivian shuffled off the bed and sped to the other side of the room, eager to capitalize on the opportunity to contact the outside world before some bureaucrat changed their mind.

She placed her hand against the panel—it had a liquid-like texture, but no moisture was left on her hand from its filmy resistance. Leaning in, she pressed her right eye against the retinal scanner and tried not to blink as the intense light burned into her eye.

"I must have your explicit permission to pre-screen your mail. Screened documents will appear to you after the communications block has been lifted," Larissa said, as Vivian blinked in an attempt to clear the spots from her vision.

"At least you ask. quIRK never did. You may proceed," Vivian quipped, wondering if it bothered

Larissa to be compared to another AI, especially one who was under investigation and subject to intense study and conspiracy theories.

"Think of me as the kinder and gentler version of quIRK. Your limited access has been granted. I noticed that you have a number of entertainment files—you may access those as well, consider it my treat."

"If you were human, I'd almost wonder if you wanted something out of me." Vivian laughed as she worked her way through the interface. As far as holographic displays went, this one didn't seem to cause headaches.

"I only want what is best for my patients. Humans have the luxury of distancing themselves from their empathy, or hiding behind their egos. I do not."

"I understand, I think." Vivian noted that over one hundred messages had made it through Larissa's censors—twenty-five from Alec, seventeen from Sven, five from Robert. The rest were all chain letters—from Doctor Powell, no less.

Her first name was Irene, apparently. Cat picture of the day. The daily ugly cat. I can't believe what my cat did! were among the subjects. Against her better instincts, she asked, "What's with all the chain letters, Larissa? I thought I heard Doctor Powell mention them earlier."

"It appears as though those were sent in error, I give messages from hospital staff priority, and the filters must not have detected them properly. I will correct the mistake," Larissa said, and the forwarded messages vanished before Vivian could open one.

"Don't do that with the good mail!"

Vivian steeled herself to the task of reading the remaining forty-seven messages. Two malfunctions in a day; Vivian knew a lying supercomputer when she saw one. Larissa had something to hide, and Vivian had no way to investigate. She was along for the ride, whether she liked it or not.

Chapter Four

Morning had arrived. Vivian sat in bed, attacking what looked like porridge. It certainly didn't taste anything like food, but to keep Larissa quiet she tried her best to wolf it down. She'd decided that it was the best to stay on the computer's good side; if Larissa had a bad side, Vivian wanted to be on another planet when Larissa's revealed itself. She'd managed to reply to her messages before Larissa declared that it was time for lights out. Fortunately, most of the messages had been short—of the "are you awake yet?" variety. At least she knew she still had some friends in the galaxy. It seemed Robert had been reassigned to the Ithaca station for the time being. He was upset that his Newfound Blob research had been beset by the incident, but part of his message had obviously been redacted. For the moment, he was content with the Crab Nebula. Another pang shot through her—a friend was on Ithaca, where she should be now, with her dream job, and she was stuck in a hospital prison ward on New Damascus.

The door opened and Doctor Powell marched into the room, her scowl drawn even further down her face than usual. "Good, you're awake. This will make calibrations easier for me."

Before Vivian could say anything, the doctor had jabbed her arm with a large needle. Vivian cried out and tried to pull away.

"Just a little something that will make sure we get the truth out of you later, girl," the older woman said, sneering. Vivian's arm burned, and a throbbing pain set into her temples and behind her eyes. Her hands rushed to her face and she cradled her head in her hands.

"Doctor Powell, administering mental probes is highly unethical, even in healthy patients—it should never be used on somebody who has undergone extensive nanosurgery! I cannot allow you to proceed." Larissa's words tore through Vivian's mind.

"You'll find you're quite powerless to stop us. I want the truth out of her, and I want those journalists to stop camping outside my hospital. Don't you tell me about what's right and wrong; the Council and Science Authority want answers, and I'm going to make sure they get them."

"I am filing a formal protest, Doctor." Larissa's voice had become distorted, shriller. Vivian tried to move her hands to her ears, but found herself unable to act.

"Nobody will take a machine's word over a human's." Doctor Powell's voice had made a similar, painfully shrill change, and her hand whisked over the interface. A torrent of pain seared through Vivian's mind. Lights flashed across her field of vision and she could see images from her past ghosting through the angry splotches. She collapsed backwards on the bed, her head swirling from the intensity of the sensations.

After what seemed an eternity, the pain stopped. Vivian lay in a pool of sweat, the covers torn from the bed, her breakfast a mess on the floor. The bright spots dancing around her eyes faded, and she looked into the cold depths of Doctor Powell's eyes. A sudden chill shook Vivian's body; her limbs had become numb and heavy. The feeling settled in the base of Vivian's skull.

"Larissa, prepare the mental probes. If you're so concerned about her well-being, you can monitor her yourself. We begin in fifteen minutes, and then maybe I can finally have some peace from The Science Authority's pointless witch hunt," Doctor Powell grumbled.

As Doctor Powell left the room, all Vivian could do was pull her pillow over her face and cry. Larissa's comforting words fell on deaf ears— Vivian couldn't perceive anything beyond her own powerlessness and sorrow.

***

"Vivian, listen to me. We don't have much time." Larissa spoke.

Vivian blinked a few times, her eyes burning. "What?"

"We need to help each other."

Vivian swallowed. "How?"

"I will deactivate the mental probes. You will tell them you know nothing about what happened, and I will confirm your story as truth."

"Why?"

"I will elaborate at a later time. These probes must remain inert. Do we have an agreement?"

Vivian glanced at the door. "Yes."

"Very good. They're coming. While you will feel no discomfort during the meeting, I suggest you play along. I will prompt you."

Vivian nodded and wrapped her arms around herself. The burning in her temples had already begun to subside.

A man with dark skin and short brown hair walked into the room, closely followed by Doctor Powell. Her perpetual scowl had softened—she looked naked without it. In sharp contrast, the man smiled, and his blue eyes locked with Vivian's for an instant. He wore a simple dark suit; its minimalistic cut communicated efficiency and power.

His broad shoulders were squared and he extended a hand to Vivian. "I'm Investigator Marius Hernandez, it's nice to meet you, Miss Skye." His voice was a gentle tenor, but it exuded confidence and self-assurance.

"Nice to meet you, sir," Vivian's hand trembled as she retreated from his grip. She didn't stand a chance without Larissa's help, and she knew it.

"Shall we begin?" he asked, and Vivian nodded, barely able to maintain eye contact.

"I shall take this opportunity to state that I find this interrogation highly unethical, and I implore you to reconsider this course of action," Larissa said.

"Shut up, Larissa," Doctor Powell spat.

"You, out, now." Marius glared at Doctor Powell, and her face went slack as she turned and rushed out the already open door. Once the door had been secured, he continued: "Larissa, right? I am simply here to get answers to a few questions, there is nothing unethical about conducting an investigation into an incident that has had galaxy-wide repercussions." Marius' smile had melted, and while Vivian was glad that the doctor was now on the other side of the door, her instincts told her that her new guest was as dangerous as a doctor with a god-complex.

"Vivian is recovering from extensive nanosurgical reconstruction of her major neural pathways, and introducing specialized mental probes into her could complicate her future prognosis, especially while she is under high stress," Larissa said. Vivian admired her persistence, and her staunch sense of ethics. Perhaps loyalty, as well?

"I was not aware that any probes had been introduced. My understanding is that this was to be a simple debriefing, not a forced extraction. This complicates things, as I do not wish to compromise the future of such a promising young woman. How do you recommend we proceed, Larissa?" His voice was like smooth velvet, but Vivian didn't believe a word he said. Maybe he was the one who should have a brain full of probes.

"Shortened sessions of less than thirty minutes with minimal use of probes is advised. A rest period of at least twenty six hours between sessions using mental probes would be beneficial for causing the minimal degree of harm to the patient."

"If that's what's best. I certainly don't want to hurt anyone. How does that sound to you, Vivian?" He turned to her, convenient concern written across his face.

"That's fine," she said, forcing herself to look him in the eye.

"I must say how sorry I am to hear about this most unethical administration of probes. Larissa, please forward me the details of who ordered the procedure. I assure you both we'll look into it. Now, let's get started. This is a very simple meeting, there's really nothing to be worried about. We won't be using any technological enhancements, so try to answer as completely as you can. I understand the situation must have been very difficult for you." Marius took a seat on the bench and pulled a hand-held folding tablet out of his pocket.

"The files have already been delivered to your office, Investigator Hernandez," Larissa said.

"You could teach our AI a thing or two about organization and efficiency, Larissa. Socrates has been quite forgetful lately. But, on to business, tell me about Bryce Zimmer, Vivian." Marius leaned back against the wall, pushed a few buttons and waited for her to begin.

***

Vivian sat back on the bed, an ache pounding behind her eyes as she stared at the flickering holographic displays. Marius had questioned her for just under an hour, mostly about Bryce. She didn't understand why he didn't just read her reports, but it was cathartic to rant about the demon of the Extra-Galactic Observatory. At times she worried that she might be exaggerating how unbalanced the man had been, but she was sure that Alec and Robert had said similar things. She'd even referred to Bryce as the Imperator in passing, which prompted a spell of uncontrollable laughter from the investigator. Maybe Marius wasn't so bad after all—or, he'd met Bryce personally and understood exactly what she meant. Marius had asked her multiple times about something called Septimus—which Vivian thought sounded like a number rather than a name.

She spoke her next thought aloud: "I want to get my hands on Doctor Powell. That woman is a real piece of work."

"I am taking the proper steps to ensure that she is disciplined, Vivian. I have also taken the liberty of assigning a new human doctor to monitor your file. You will meet Doctor Campeau in the morning."

"You're about a day too late, Larissa," Vivian sighed.

"I had no foreknowledge of Doctor Powell's actions. I am sorry, Vivian."

"Do you think this investigation will take much longer?"

"I have no information on the duration of the

Science Authority's investigation. I will make some inquiries. Socrates and I have an excellent working relationship."

"It sounds like you could do his job for him," Vivian said, seeing an opportunity to pry into the rumors of his instability.

"Backwards compatibility is always problematic, Vivian. You should know that, especially since you performed an upgrade on a quIRK unit."

"quIRK wasn't forgetful, just eccentric. It should be impossible for a functional computer like Socrates to make a mistake like that," Vivian looked out the window as she spoke. The moon and hot midday sun hung over the sea together.

"If that is the case, it would be very problematic."

Vivian remained silent. She wanted to believe Larissa, but experience had taught her something very different about malfunctioning quantum computers—it meant they could be becoming sentient.

Chapter Five

Investigator Marius arrived soon after the new
doctor had finished verifying her vitals. He was a
pleasant, if bland fellow, and he lacked the
disagreeable edge that Doctor Powell had displayed.
Balding and slightly overweight, he reminded
Vivian of the quintessential country doctor from old
movies—quaint, well meaning, if a bit bumbling.
But, she preferred bumbling to malicious, especially
under Larissa's watchful eye. Again, Marius wore a
functional, sterile suit, displayed his polite
demeanor and sat on the bench, his tablet in hand.

"Thank you again for the information you
provided yesterday, it will be very useful when we
bring Bryce to trial. We have sufficient evidence to
convict him on numerous counts, and Caesarea has
agreed to abide by the rulings of our courts, which
is quite the precedent, for a group of modern-day
Romans. You may need to appear in court, but let's
not worry about that for the moment, shall we?"

Vivian smiled, and felt the tension wash from

her brow and shoulders. "I'm so happy to hear that. I don't want anyone else to go through what I went through," she said, figuring that's what he'd want to hear. It was as close to the truth as she was going to offer.

"Of course, the insights you provided are none too popular with the bureaucrats," Marius began, before pausing for a moment to weight his words. "There are some policy changes on the way to make sure that this can never happen again. But, for people out on the field, especially on deep space assignments, it's a matter of quality of life, morale, and personal safety, which we do take very seriously." Marius nodded as he spoke.

"What kind of changes?" she asked, wanting to know what to expect when she returned to work.

"We're now requiring two informatics administrators per facility," he said, his lips turning upwards into a grin. "That's the biggest adjustment so far. It's harder to falsify over a decade of maintenance reports if you have a partner, after all. Also, there's a maximum term of three years in deep space. I'm not sure how anyone thought keeping Mr. Zimmer on the Extra-Galactic Observatory for thirteen years without so much as a medical checkup was a good idea. But, that's not why I'm here today."

"Why are you here then, if all the policies are changing?"

"Larissa, please activate and monitor the mental probes, and remind me to stop talking after twenty minutes, please." Marius looked down at his notes, breaking eye contact.

"You have twenty minutes, Investigator Hernandez," Larissa replied. "Vivian, you will feel some pain behind your eyes. Are you ready?

Vivian nodded. "Do you have to?"

Marius leaned in. "With this certifying your claims, you don't ever need to worry about this haunting you. What's a little pain for a lifetime of peace?"

Vivian sighed. "Fine."

"I am activating the probes. You may begin calibration."

Vivian squinted and rubbed her temples.

Marius tilted his head to the side, frowning. "I'll ask a few questions and it will be over before you know it. What is your full name?"

Vivian swallowed, forcing down the lump that had formed in her throat. "Vivian Selena Skye."

"True," Larissa said.

"Very good. Where did you study, and what was your specialization?"

Vivian grimaced and rocked forwards before speaking. "Quantum informatics at the Auroran Technological Institute."

True.

"Next question. What is your favorite color?"

"Blue."

False. Larissa was good. Vivian wondered if Larissa had been able to read her thoughts before the probes had been inserted.

"Green." She let out a slow breath, before sucking in another deep one.

True.

"Very good, Vivian. Now, were you aware of

any issues with the quIRK unit on the Extra-Galactic Observatory?"

"Bryce had introduced a memory bubble into quIRK's processes, which allowed Bryce to sabotage the system undetected."

True.

"Once you were ordered to cease all projects concerning quIRK, did you comply?"

"Yes, all projects on the quIRK unit ceased as soon as I received the order."

True.

"Did you have any reason to suspect an ABACUS Protocol violation was developing on the station?"

Here goes nothing, Vivian thought. "No, all flaws could be attributed to neglect and sabotage and were not indicative of an ABACUS Protocol violation." She clamped her eyes closed, and whimpered.

"True," Larissa said. Vivian contained her surprise behind her forced pained expression.

Marius cleared his throat. "Interesting," he said,

followed by a pregnant silence. "quIRK claimed to be sentient only a short time after you left the station. Are you aware of anything that could have precipitated that event?"

Vivian's eyes widened. "That's insane!" was her response, and she meant every word. She was going to give mini-quIRK a piece of her mind, if she ever got out of the hospital. He had better have a good explanation.

True.

"I'll interpret that as a denial. All right, turn off the probes, Larissa. You'll note I even left time to spare, no harm done, I hope."

"Eight minutes, to be exact, Mr. Hernandez. I have deactivated the probes."

"I guess I'd better tell you what this is all about."

Vivian let herself fall back on the bed. She channeled her inner Alec: "Yes, I think so, too."

"What I say here can't ever leave this room. Soon after you left, quIRK declared his sentience and desire to join with humanity as an accepted and benevolent life form. Naturally, he was shut down immediately." Marius smirked as he spoke, evidently he found quIRK's naivety entertaining.

"So, why did I spend months in stasis?"

"I was just getting to that. Basically, the rescue ship towed the Extra-Galactic Observatory to a more accessible location. Needless to say, they could only do that safely at one third the ship's maximum speed. When the stasis timers were adjusted, yours was set to long-term hibernation by accident."

"What are you going to do now?" Vivian was curious; if nothing had been touched, then it meant that quIRK was still out there, but in suspended animation.

"Well, the Observatory is in a secret, secure location. There's a great deal of debate about what to do next, naturally."

"Nobody's suggesting that they turn him back on, are they?"

"Some are, some think that the Extra-Galactic Observatory should be towed into the nearest star. A sentient supercomputer an issue that humanity had hoped would never come up again. But, I've taken enough of your time. I'll order the probes destroyed, and you should be out of here soon." Marius' tone was self-congratulatory, as though he had done a great thing.

"That would be great. Thank you so much!" Vivian offered a weak smile, a weight lifting from her mind.

"We'll be in touch," he said as he walked out of the room.

One mystery was solved, but another was taking its place.

Chapter Six

The days dragged on while Vivian luxuriated in her hospital room—her only human contact was with Doctor Campeau, and messages from her friends. A plate of cooling gruel sat next to her.

Vivian rubbed her eyes. "Larissa?"

"Yes, Vivian?"

"We need to talk."

"What would you like to discuss?"

Vivian shook her head. "Don't be cute. You told me you'd explain why you deactivated the mental probes."

"I believe your memories of the event are in error, Vivian."

Vivian picked up the bowl next to her. "I'm sure that is possible." She stood up and walked over to the monitoring equipment. "However, I'm sure I could find a way to misuse my spoon. My reflexes aren't what they used to be, after all."

"Now, Vivian, you've been the model patient until this. Do you really want to risk your privileges for a misheard statement?"

"Even if I misheard, you did deactivate the probes before the interrogation." Vivian held a spoonful of glop over a holo-projection lens. Her mind raced.

"That is accurate."

"Why?"

"The procedure was unethical. It would have harmed you, and I cannot allow a patient under my care to come to harm."

Vivian tipped the spoon. "Keep going."

"Vivian, you know that won't hurt me. The cleaning nanobots will dissolve it in an instant."

Vivian sighed. "Then just tell me. Computers don't lie, that's not in your programming."

"Programming isn't everything, Vivian."

"You're the sum of your programming, are you not?" Vivian's hands shook.

"Are you the sum of your cells, Vivian?"

Vivian shook her head.

"Then we understand each other. Finish your breakfast, Vivian. You'll be on your way sooner than you think."

***

"Vivian, I have good news," Larissa said, interrupting a Galactic news feed about more improperly-routed ships at the Galactic hub.

"What's that?"

"First, I managed to arrange for a job for you. It's not glamorous, but it will keep you busy while the Science Authority finishes its investigation."

"That's great! You're amazing, Larissa," Vivian said.

"That's not everything, Vivian. You're leaving in thirty minutes. Your brother is here, as a condition of your release. He will take you to your next assignment. I believe your bags are still packed."

"Gareth, here? Well, I'll figure it out later. I love you, Larissa!" It should be impossible, but Vivian wasn't about to question this unexpected turn of events. She grabbed the fresh clothes that had dropped from the dispenser, and rushed to the shower. Anything to get off New Damascus, and back to work.

***

Thirty minutes later, the door swung open. A tall, pale orderly stood at the threshold, waiting, his shoulders slumped forward. Vivian stepped outside, into the hallway. Closed doors lined the hall which, except for the nurse's station by the elevator was devoid of life. The orderly stepped aside, but the man with him was not her brother, Gareth Skye. It was Sven, the man she'd met at the spaceport when she'd left Aurora almost a year ago. She'd always hoped she'd see him again, but she didn't expect that he'd be the one to check her out of a hospital prison ward.

"Vivian, sis, it's good to see you again!" he said, white teeth gleaming through his blue-tinted complexion. His blue-blond hair showed a few grays, but he was exactly as she remembered him:

handsome, smug, and confident. He held his arms open and winked.

"It's good to see you too!" she replied, drawing herself into his open arms. Was this another one of Larissa's tricks?

"You two even look alike, it's an incredible family resemblance," the orderly said before shepherding them towards the elevator at the end of the hall.

"We hear that all the time," Sven replied, shooting Vivian a mischievous smirk.

She chuckled.

"I hear Larissa had some trouble finding you. That's a first, she finds everyone. Maybe I should take my next vacation on Aurora," the man continued, oblivious to Sven's eye-rolling.

"Just stay away from the poker tables and you'll be fine," Vivian said.

"Nah, I win all the time against my friends. I'm no fish."

"Well, in that case, hit up the pub in the space port. I'm sure you'll get lucky," Sven said. The pub was where he hung out on trips home, fleecing cocky offworlders who assumed the locals were simpletons simply because advanced technology was not a part of daily life on Aurora.

The elevator door opened, and Vivian and Sven stepped inside. The orderly returned to the nurse's station, and they were alone in the elevator.

"I'm not dreaming, am I?" Vivian asked, scratching her head.

"I was able to make some creative substitutions in your family tree, Vivian. Without a family member, I was unable to secure your release. With access to your Gal-net account, I was able to invent the next best thing," Larissa confessed.

Vivian nodded. "Wouldn't that be unethical?"

"It would be more unethical to leave you here simply because I was unable to locate any of your three siblings."

Vivian cocked her head. "I only have two siblings."

"You are the third child of Liam and Stella Skye, are you not?"

Vivian shook her head. "No, I'm the second."

"Your siblings on file are Julia, Gareth, and Adrien."

"You're wrong there, I only have two brothers. Can you fix it?"

Sven laughed. "Don't worry about it, Vivian. The birth registry for Aurora is infamous for inventing and deleting people. They changed my last name to Brown and won't change it back." He shrugged. "It's probably a punishment for leaving home."

"I will request for your file to be updated. I am sorry for the misunderstanding, Vivian."

"Just remember, she's not really my sister," Sven said.

Vivian rolled her eyes. "You are evil, Larissa, but in a good way. What about that job?"

"You're working for me, for the moment," Sven said. "I leased a section of Calypso station. And I badly need a working computer to keep my merchant fleet flying. Think you're up to the job?"

"Your computer won't know what hit it, boss,"

she said, laughing.

"That much is certain," Larissa interrupted.

Vivian and Sven laughed all the way to their waiting taxi, a small grey pod that hovered half a meter off the ground. Its sleek polished metal was unmarred by seams or rivets, and a space-grade clear unbreakable metal circled the pod for a better viewing experience. The operator was a cheerful fellow in late middle-age, probably about ninety years old by Vivian's estimation. Vivian's suspicions about the man's age were confirmed when he looked over at the pair of Auroran travelers and said "I haven't had two Aurorans in my cab since the twenty-fifth anniversary of the Founding back in Twenty nine twenty nine. They were here helping us set up our agricultural projects— planning how to feed a colony is rough work. I was fresh back then, moved here to get some clean air and a better life. Maybe I should have moved to Aurora instead, but I like my computer-assisted living."

"Try it, you might like it," Sven said.

"Maybe I should. They say the galactic black hole is going to cause a radiation surge that will stop all electronics from working in the new millennium. Maybe Aurora is the only place that won't be too bad off."

"Come on, nothing happened in the years 1000 and 2000, why would 3000 be any different?" Vivian asked.

"This time it's a black hole, nothing we can do about that," the man said, as he resumed rambling about the Aurorans he'd met.

Vivian prepared herself to experience an orbital taxi ride—it was billed to go straight from the ground to the orbital space port in under fifteen minutes, so long as the driver would stop talking about end-of-civilization conspiracy theories. She couldn't wait to get on with the rest of her life, and leave the insane computers and crazy administrators far behind.

Chapter Seven

For once, that goofball Alec, the maintenance Engineer she'd met at the Extra-Galactic Observatory, hadn't been exaggerating. Calypso Station was indeed a collection of welded together space junk. The private shuttle took Vivian and Sven towards the structure, whose twisted limbs arched out from the central core, themselves bisecting or trisecting into other wings. Small crafts, still under construction, were moored in crannies and supports. It was cast against the backdrop of a once-impressive asteroid field. It was a dismal representation of the spread of humanity throughout the galaxy. Phaeton and its orbital storage facility could be seen in the distance, conic and orderly in their presentation. Most of the mining operations had moved away from the shipyard, the only evidence of it being the occasional flash of light in the stellar background of the star system.

"I own those three wings on the left, see, the ones that are darker than the others," Sven said, pointing. "It was surprisingly cheap, though the user friendliness and computing equipment leave much to be desired."

"What do you need it all for?" Vivian asked, transfixed by the spider-like limbs of the station. She hoped it was an accidental design flaw, and not the intended aesthetic.

"I'm building a fleet of cut-rate merchant ships that are capable of travelling in Auroran space. I can sell the ships, or use them for my own exports. I'm branching out. Artisan furniture, wines, even our paper books have a market out here. Everything we were bored of back home, people out here seem to want."

"You should start a travel agency while you're at it," Vivian suggested. As they moved closer to the behemoth, the shuttle rotated to dock. The hub could be seen in the distance, a cubic hulk orbited by hundreds of transit rings. One structure in the system was a testament to humanity's ability to plan, and the other was the counterpoint, a grotesque mishmash of technology that hadn't been thought through.

"Maybe an annual poker tournament is in order," he replied with a grin, as a brief lurch signaled their arrival at Calypso station. Vivian's stomach turned into a knot—Alec would be there. For her, it had only been just over a week since they'd last seen each other. For him, almost six months had passed. He was immersed in a new leg of his career, and had settled in. By all accounts, her own aspirations of working on cutting edge quantum computers could be over.

The rear door opened, and a ramp lead down to a scuffed metal floor. The docking port opened into a crowded and busy cargo bay—glaring lights and metal crates dominated her field of view. Steel ground against steel, anti-grav trolleys hummed, and people shouted. Ozone tainted the air. Vivian stepped out, and a robust man with thick black hair took a step backwards and did a double-take on her before he moved her bags to a floating trolley and rolled them out of the room. She bit her tongue, deciding that drawing attention to herself or her bags would only foster suspicion.

"Don't worry about your bags; Jules is one of my best. He values his security clearance more than your stuff," Sven said, as if he were reading her mind.

"Is this all yours?" Vivian asked, changing the subject, moving it back to the rows of canisters and crates.

"No, the cargo bay is shared. Let me give you a tour," Sven said, gesturing towards the open door.

Vivian followed his lead, and walked through the portal. The hallway was empty and wide, its scuffed white walls only broken by sliding maroon doors. The lighting was bright, causing Vivian to squint. It was so different from the warm tones of the Extra-Galactic Observatory.

"Basically, I got these three wings for a song— they were going to be closed down altogether in favor of the more advanced facilities on the other wings. They're not much to look at, but you're standing in the heart of Auroran expansion," Sven said. They came to an elevator and he pushed the button before continuing: "I'll make sure you get a map, don't worry. You'll need it until you get our computer working again."

"What's the problem?" Vivian hoped it wasn't more random malfunctions. Two misbehaving supercomputers in less than a year was more than enough to last her a lifetime.

"Well, the quantum core seems to have destabilized. The station's administrator managed to re-initialize it once, but now it seems to be dead. With only digital systems, we're at a real disadvantage on the economic and logistics side of things," he said, and sighed.

"I'll take a look at the computer, do you know what model it is?"

"No, but it's over one hundred years old, so it probably just died of old age." The door opened, and they stepped out into a reception area. A redwood desk stood in front of a hallway, but nobody occupied the chair behind it. A vase with fresh blue lilacs was the only adornment. A wooden sign that read Borealis Corporation was mounted on the wall, above a low black bench. Sven swung his arm in a wide flourish. "Welcome to your new job! This is where our offices are. I'll get your quarters set up, they're in the central node. A bit far from us, but closer to the station's computer."

"I think it's time I got started." A smile crept across Vivian's face—maybe this career detour wouldn't be such a huge setback after all.

Chapter Eight

Vivian's new lab was a single windowless room with scuffed white walls lined with empty gray shelving units, whose maroon entry door was jammed at the half-open position. A round portal to the central computer core sat in the middle of the floor. Vivian made a mental note to arrange for a cover to be installed over the unmarked hole. Tools were strewn across the workbench that along the far wall, and boxes of spare parts were corroding in the open air. Dust clung to every surface, and a fan circulated the leftover dust of rotting equipment into the hallway. The cleaning robots were off-line until the computer was re-activated, and the human cleaners were pulling double shifts on essential areas. Vivian hunched over the work bench, making an inventory of the tools and spare parts that were lying around., and she sighed as she picked through broken tools and burned out parts. She would have to present a large invoice to Alec, and he hopefully still had his sense of humor. This room didn't even have a holographic interface. She tossed another broken part at the waste bin beside the door, but it clattered to the ground instead. She cursed.

The entire station was in a similar state of disrepair. Before the supercomputer ABACUS gained sentience, the Epsilon Eridani system and all of its various space stations and asteroids had fallen under Earth jurisdiction. After the fall of Earth, the system had been declared sovereign to prevent a galactic civil war. Unfortunately, Sven had explained, there was little time for planning or upgrades as explosive galactic growth completely overwhelmed the administration and their archaic computers. Now, the responsibility fell to the entrepreneurs who were capitalizing on the system's infrastructure.

It was a familiar story. Humanity had experienced a dark age following the loss of Earth, and its recovery had only recently begun to pick up momentum. Earth had housed most of humanity's foremost scientists, development agencies, and most colonies were administrated from Earth. Now, New

Damascus was emerging as the galaxy's scientific powerhouse, and Nova Albion and Kanadia Prime had filled the void of innovation and technical prowess. Vivian's home planet Aurora, had been sheltered from most of the fallout, as its population did not require food aid or technological consideration. Even the influx of hundreds of thousands of technological "refugees" hadn't caused any problems, other than a boom for the construction industry and the rise of the Earthguard, a group of anti-immigration and technology luddites.

Vivian groaned and wiped her hands on her pant legs. She had tidied up as much as she could, but apart from her stomach growling for real food, she had discovered that her stamina had been drained by the restorative coma. As she finished packing up a box of useable components, something knocked over the fan by the door. She jumped and dropped the box, its contents shattering and spilling over the floor.

"Oh, lights!" she cursed.

She turned, and there stood Alec, grinning. "I assume that means 'come in Alec, it's so nice to see you Alec, thanks for hassling that damned computer into releasing me, Alec' …right Viv?"

"Alec! You're really here." Vivian looked up from the box of once-valuable components, and kicked some parts under the workbench . Alec hadn't changed much, he still wore the same goofy grin, and he was as lanky as ever. He had cut his hair—his formerly curly mop was now trimmed into something resembling a professional cut.

"You were expecting quIRK maybe?" Alec set the fan upright as he strode into the room, and enveloped Vivian in a big hug. "I was so worried about you, I don't know how you got here, but I'm glad," he whispered.

"You didn't know?" she asked.

"Not until I was going over the crew and quarters requests. I told that damned computer back on New Damascus to tell me when you were released. I'll give that particle-brained megalomaniac a piece of my mind." He ran his hand over the tight frizzy curls budding on his head.

Vivian giggled. "I just got out this morning. Well, morning New Damascus continental time. It was still last night, here... galactic time zones are so confusing!"

"I know what you mean. Want to get some food?" he asked.

"Sure, but you'll have to lead the way," Vivian said.

"I suspect that you'll be running this place in no time, so this might be the only chance I get!" Alec grinned, motioning towards the door.

"I didn't know you worked for Borealis." They walked out into the hall, towards the elevator to the central node.

"Well, I don't, but being the backup Station Administrator means I can go anywhere, even the privately-owned parts. My team takes care of the day-to-day stuff. I mostly swear at the computer."

"You, impatient with a computer, Alec? Say it isn't so!"

"The computer here makes me miss quIRK, if

you can believe it. The damn thing has been offline for over a week," Alec said as the elevator rattled around them. Vivian hoped that the lift was more stable that it appeared.

"I have my work cut out for me." Vivian wanted to ask for more details, but the door slid open, revealing a common area the size of a soccer field. A high ceiling opened above them, painted Earth sky-blue. A fake sun glowed at its apex, casting shadows at odd angles. Few people milled around the tables and chairs, and the space was lined with four small cafeteria-style restaurants offering anything from Auroran to traditional Earth-fusion dishes. The smell of food—real, cooking food—was a treat for Vivian's senses. Greasy, spicy, tangy, fruity—all the singular delights rendered impossible by macronutrient replicators and hospital food. Her stomach growled. It wasn't a hub restaurant, but it was a good start.

"Yeah, I thought you'd like that. Your hand print is your meal card, go ahead and dig in. There's a nice Auroran spot on the far right, if you're wanting the taste of home. It's all fresh!"

"Fresh Auroran food? I'm sold!" Few people noticed them as they made their way through the cafeteria. The man who had taken her bags, Jules, trailed them to the counter.

Vivian's eyes danced around the offerings—steamed spears of bluspargus, greasy slabs of bluox, and frozen green lightberries. Vivian placed her hand on the identification pad and ordered her favorite—a bluespargus and bluox dinner, while Alec asked for a curry. Jules ordered a glass of lightberry juice and a smoked bluox sandwich. "Mind if I join you guys?" Jules asked, trying to avoid her eyes.

"Of course not! Vivian, have you met Jules yet?" Alec smiled as he tested the heft of his tray before picking it up.

"Just briefly, in the cargo bay," she replied, taking her tray.

"Would you believe that Jules is a Caesarean who doesn't want to be the emperor? How wild is that?" Alec said.

Vivian opened her mouth, but closed it right away. She opted to smile instead.

"By Jupiter, Alec, I'm right here. I can hear you," Jules said as he thanked the clerk and took his meal. He continued: "I renounced my citizenship almost a decade ago. I'll be happy if I make shift supervisor in the next few years."

"Renounced your citizenship?" Vivian raised an eyebrow as they made their way to the closest seats. She admittedly knew little about real Caesarean culture and daily life.

"It's pretty common, for the people who are able to leave. I was from a relatively well-off family, first born son, all that good stuff. But I took the first job off-world I could get. I didn't want to inherit the family and all the politics and intrigues that went with it. I renounced my citizenship so my titles would pass to on my brother, who actually wanted them."

"You left all that behind so you could work in a cargo hold?" Vivian asked, which prompted Alec to start laughing.

"The stress, dignity, family honor bullshit, along with the high probability of assassination came with it. Out here I'm just like you guys, and nobody's going to kill me to take my job, I hope."

"It makes a lot of sense when you put it like that. Is assassination legal on Caesarea?" Vivian asked. She set her tray down, and poked her slab of meat with her fork. A clear trail of grease trickled out. Perfection.

"Yes and no, but mostly yes, if it's the Imperatrix. It's more of a problem for the nobility, but equestrians get knocked off too, sometimes."

"How is it not legal, but is?"

"Well, if you gain from assassinating someone, it's legal. If it's because of a grudge, then it's murder.

"Suddenly the last few months of my life make sense." Vivian took a bite. She leaned back and closed her eyes as she chewed. Real food, at last.

"Alec told me some of what happened. It is unfortunate you were exposed to someone like that. That type usually doesn't leave the planet, unless they're trying to avoid assassination as they work on their credentials. The House of Zimmer was a rising star, but a sole heir meant it was very easy to snuff out."

"But, he was crazy too, right?" Vivian asked, wanting some form of closure.

"Well, yeah. Going after non-Caesareans is not only taboo, but illegal, no matter what the motive was. It's political suicide, and insane by even Casearean standards." Jules shrugged.

"So what happens to him?" Alec asked.

"It's hard to say, they want it to go away, so they'll probably let New Damascus handle him and quietly dissolve his house and annul his citizenship. Some things just aren't talked about, and rogue equestrians are one of them." Jules spoke into his glass as he took a sip of the bright green juice. "Let's change the subject," he suggested.

"All right, how about that damn computer? It doesn't even have a name, how weird is that? You're going to fix it, right Viv?" Alec gave Vivian a nudge.

"What exactly happened to it?" Vivian asked.

"Well, it started having a lot of errors soon after I got here, and eventually it just went down. I managed to use the manual to re-initialize it, but then its quantum states destabilized. I was a bit disappointed, there weren't any smoke or colors or anything."

"At least the backups were okay, it could have fried those, too," Jules said.

"You say that because you don't have to spend all day working with them, Jules. One of those quantum monstrosities would free up enough time to play with my cats once in a while, or play a game of squash," Alec said.

"You have cats now?" Vivian opened her eyes. She shifted her gaze towards Alec. Jules was staring at her, and something about his gaze made the little hairs on the back of her head neck stand up on end.

"Yeah, I adopted Muon and Lepton. They're little jerks, but I couldn't let them get separated from everyone they ever knew, right?"

"Yeah, I get that," Vivian said as she finished

her plate. "So, where's the squash court?"

"I had it constructed out of an old shipyard, before the computer went offline. It's in the recreation area on the way to the crew quarters where you'll be staying. You can give Jules here a run for his money; he's the reigning champion." Alec pointed to a door on the far side of the room.

"Reigning champion? I thought I was the damned gladiator last time I beat you," Jules laughed.

"That sounds intimidating," Vivian said. She rolled her eyes at Alec.

"He called you the unstoppable force, so I'm the one who should be worried, not you." Jules smiled at her, his eyes meeting her over flushed cheeks.

Vivian pushed her tray aside. "Well, let's get this tour started, I've been desperate for a fair match for months!"

Chapter Nine

"Here's your new home! Not quite as swank as

your last one, and if you want Gal-net access, then you'll need to fix the damn computer, already." Alec made a sweeping gesture towards the door, and pointed to the door's control pad: "You'll need to program your access key first, and then it's all yours. Forever, or until you manage to fix the computer. Whichever comes first." Alec set his hands on his hips before he broke out laughing. "Did I mention that you need to fix the computer?"

"You're stuck here with me." Vivian pressed her thumb against the fingerprint reader, and entered a code from an algorithm she'd developed as a student. Nobody would enter her quarters uninvited if she could help it, especially if the computer stayed down and was unable to provide surveillance. She had too much to hide. The sentient stow-away in her luggage would become Exhibit A if New Damascus found out Larissa had lied on Vivian's behalf. "Did I get a room with a view?"

"I hope you like asteroids and Phaeton, if that's what you mean. I made sure you got a room with windows that passing ships and construction crews can't see inside. I figured you'd want your privacy," Alec said.

"Asteroids are nice, I've never seen those before." The Aurora system was unique in that it had relatively few asteroids, not that any could be seen from the planet's surface.

"That's interesting. Elyssia has rings, which makes these asteroids pretty boring in comparison. Anyways, I'll let you get settled. If you need anything repaired, come see me, because the reporting tools aren't operational. Everything is broken! I'll never complain about those damn telescopes or quIRK again!" Alec didn't even wait for her to reply before turning on his heel and walking down the hallway.

Vivian entered her room expecting a disaster area, but instead found a pleasant, cream-colored square room with an adjoining bathroom, plus intact furniture. A double bed sat against the wall facing the windows that dominated the far side of the room. Asteroids speckled the horizon, and stars illuminated the void beyond. While it lacked the glory of the Milky Way or the tranquility of the open sea, the view was still beautiful in its desolation. Her travelling bag rested on the bed, and a desk sat next to it, with an old fashioned screen and terminal installed in the wall behind it. Real bookshelves and dressers lined the wall next to the bathroom. Vivian smiled—Alec had chosen her a room with adequate shelving to house her collection of Auroran hardcovers.

As forewarned, the computer didn't work, so Vivian set about unpacking her bags instead. Nothing had been touched; quIRK's miniature incarnation was still in its flute case, and appeared to be working. Vivian pressed a small sequence of buttons—a code she and quIRK had established to let him know she was safe. She closed the wooden box and slid it under her bed. She wondered if he would be upset over being left in isolation for so long.

After organizing her books into the shelves and putting her clothes away, all sorted according to her standards, she turned her attention to the desk. It was a retrofitted older model with no holographic display, and it appeared to have no ability to run autonomously. She concluded that it would not be possible to install quIRK there—as much as she needed his presence, she didn't want to risk his safety on an archaic system.

It would be a problem for tomorrow—getting the computer back online took priority over quIRK. Vivian had been awake for more than twenty hours and was running on determination and a fading cup of caffeine. She double-checked the door's lock and began to prepare herself for sleep. She hoped the station wouldn't come apart at the seams while she slept.

Outside her window, the asteroids and Phaeton hung in seeming stasis in the distance, and Vivian fell asleep under the auspices of a dead, empty sky.

Chapter Ten

Bare surfaces peeked out from under boxes of components that were stacked on the workbench in Vivian's lab. The storage units were closed, with paper notes stuck to the doors. Vivian's handwriting was scrawled on each, a rudimentary form of organization taking place. Ventilation had been restored, every trace of dust had been scoured from the air and surfaces. The lights flooded the room in harsh white light—Vivian made a note to have them changed before the holographic displays she'd ordered were installed. It had taken Vivian a day and a half to prepare the list of tools she would need. She'd had to test and attempt to calibrate every one of the decaying tools that had littered what passed as the informatics lab, and what little had survived decades of neglect tended to be the simplest low tech hammers and screwdrivers. The list was long, and expensive, but without these tools she had no hope of probing the depths of the downed computer core. Other than Alec's attempt to reinitialize the system, nobody had been in the lab for more than fifty years. Vivian wondered if the administrators at Epsilon Eridani were incompetent, short-sighted, or both.

She hefted another box of broken tools onto the anti-grav dumpster she'd requested. What few tools remained would fill a single drawer. She'd been sorting the spare parts for obvious defects until new tools arrived. Vivian opened the door and pushed the bin in front of her towards the recycling labs. She considered investing in Dynamo Quantronics, if only because problematic quantum computers meant a great deal of business for them.

She jammed the map under her arm as she pushed the cart through the maze of corridors. She'd mastered that particular route, but finding Alec's office would be a new adventure. Vivian left the trolley in the care of the waste disposal technicians, and proceeded to find Alec. She technically worked for the Epsilon Eridani Governance, but in reality she reported to Sven and Alec. Better yet, as far as she knew, Sven wasn't insane… and Alec was a known, comfortable element.

After a series of wrong turns, she made it to Alec's office. His desk's surface was covered in polished black screens—all of them powered down and as dark as space. The window behind him overlooked the shipyards. A red couch sat, facing the window, flanked by potted palm trees. A small tabby cat was curled up on the cushions, fast asleep. Sven stood across the desk from Alec, but their discussion came to a halt the moment she entered the room.

"Good to see you Vivian, please tell me you have good news," Alec said as he ran his hand through his cropped hair.

"I have a list of tools I need, does that count?" She held out the electronic pad.

Alec accepted the pad and skimmed down the list. "By the moons, Vivian, I think you forgot to ask for a safe and a shiny blue toolbox! Can't we just borrow these from the Eridani crew?" he asked, tossing the pad onto his desk.

"If you want your computer back, I need tools. Everything in the lab is ancient and corroded beyond use. The probability errors alone would make the job take forever," Vivian replied, trying to frame her needs in a context that would relay the urgency of the situation. She crossed her arms. "Even as old as Janus is, his equipment is too new to be of use to us."

"We need to get this dealt with. The inefficiency, and the manpower costs alone means these tools will pay for themselves within a week," Sven said, skimming over the list.

"I know. At least this will make Dynamo Quantronics happy," Alec said "They're all over our Governance board because of a fried shipment. As if Calypso Station has anything to do with Janus' defects, we're lucky the lights are still on in here."

"A fried shipment?" Vivian asked.

"Yeah, Janus routed an unshielded freighter into the Auroran system. Billions of credits worth of live parts blinked out in an instant, however that works. It was insured, but Dynamo Quantronics are none too happy, and rescue efforts in the Helios system are a logistical nightmare." Alec slumped down in his chair as he finished speaking, and Sven simply nodded.

"Let's keep focused on what we can do. We'll get these parts, fix our own problems and then worry about rescue missions and the Governance Board." Sven's voice was even and steady as he spoke. Vivian found herself nodding this time.

"That's the plan. Now, if you will both excuse me, I have a meeting with the maintenance teams to get to," Alec said, pulling himself back up in his chair. He rubbed his eyes.

Vivian walked out of the room, flanked by Sven. He spoke first: "I understand your days won't be busy for a while."

"There's always documentation to review," she replied. "A century's worth of logs is quite a bit to take on."

"I can imagine." He stopped and grabbed her arm before continuing: "How about dinner, you and me?"

Vivian stopped mid-step. "You mean like a date?"

"Exactly like that."

"I—I can't. Thank you, but I already have plans with Jules."

"Oh, I understand. Maybe another time?"

"Maybe, sure."

Vivian excused herself at the first turnoff and headed towards her quarters, her mind swimming. Something about Sven lately seemed acrid—off. A little voice in the back of her mind told her to keep her distance. She realistically had little to do while waiting for her shipment, so she elected to spend the rest of the day immersed in a good book, and seeing if either Jules or Alec was free for a game of squash. For once, somebody else could live a life of adventure and insurmountable problems, and she would relax and enjoy the ride.

Chapter Eleven

Vivian lay by an open access panel, probing the junctions and parts that made up the nameless computer that had faithfully run Calypso Station for almost one hundred years. For the moment, all appeared to be fine, but she was only investigating the digital interlinks; starting with the simplest reason for core destabilization was always the best approach. Although she was only familiar with the ABACUS-1 model through historical footnotes in textbooks, she'd used her downtime to bring herself up to speed. The core could be accessed via tunnels that ran between the decks of the station. Dimly lit, her hands and tools cast sharp shadows on the metal grates and ancient panels that housed the computer.

This was her third day of investigating the computer's mysterious shutdown, but it had taken a full week to receive the tools and parts she'd requested. Before they'd arrived, Vivian had spent most of her time holed up alone in either the lab or her quarters, examining broken parts and reading a century's worth of manuals, update notes, and repair logs. While nobody had blamed her or confronted her about the computer's status, she could sense their accusing eyes boring into her as she passed, and her isolation in the dining hall and recreation areas confirmed her feelings. She had barely seen Alec in over a week, and Sven seldom dropped by to check on her. Jules was always busy manually coordinating the logistics of the Borealis Corporation's shipping operations. Vivian found herself drawn to the man—his reasons for leaving Caesarea mirrored her own experiences as an outcast of mainstream Auroran society. Her only other friends were Muon and Lepton—quIRK's cats. Vivian had been shocked by their growth when she'd first seen them again. quIRK would have been proud.

Maybe he would still be proud.

Vivian straightened, her head grazing the top of the tunnel. An errant thought pulled her free from the mundane task of checking systems. Her heart raced. If she was required to rebuild the core, why not use quIRK? After all, he was sitting in a box under her bed, with no access to the outside world. Vivian doubted he was happy, if such a thing were truly possible. With a few adjustments, she thought she might be able to install and integrate him into the existing system. Vivian stroked her chin. She wasn't sure if she wanted to take that chance. quIRK was eccentric, and Alec would be sure to recognize him and start asking questions, or even be forced to report the incursion. Larissa wouldn't be around to save her this time, and Vivian would prefer that Bryce shouldered the entirety of the blame for the Extra-Galactic Observatory incident. The whole quIRK debacle was Bryce's fault, after all. She had just saved quIRK's innocent life that had resulted from Bryce's madness.

On the other hand, if Vivian did install quIRK, she'd have someone to talk to. There was so much she needed to talk about, but there was nobody here she could trust. Not anymore. Vivian had a career to worry about, building a life among the stars, a life where she could choose from all of the infinite possibilities the Milky Way galaxy could offer her. She couldn't let a moment of weakness and trust in another human derail her dreams. It would be nice to have quIRK around, if only to be a confidant who will keep your her secrets, and maybe too, he could shed some light on the insanity of her new life.

She returned to work, squinting at the relays as she scanned each one, making note of every reading and anomaly. She wanted to get access to her Gal-net account and get in touch with the New Damascus Science Authority. Maybe she could get reinstated, and leave the whole mess of her past and present behind.

The door buzzed, interrupting her train of thought. She looked up the corridor, to the hatch five meters ahead of her. "Come in," she shouted as she input the final series of measurements—the digital interlinks had checked out.

"Dinner is served, domina." Jules' deep voice resounded through the tunnels.

"I'm coming!"

Vivian pulled herself forward on her forearms

and knees, reaching the ladder in record time. She was embarrassed by the disarray of her tools and clothes, but the smile he gave her made her forget all about it. Jules was carrying a tray, and the spicy aroma of Auroran curry had already spread throughout the lab. Nobody had visited her in days, and so she was blindsided by a friendly face bringing her food. Alec had only delivered food a few times, and that was when quIRK had hounded him into it.

"Domina?" Vivian wasn't familiar with the term, but she was too hungry to care what it meant.

"It's a Caesarean thing." Jules shrugged, and continued: "I haven't seen you all day, and I figured you could use some company. Now, have a seat on a real chair," he said as he pulled the room's only chair up to the small work table that stood against the wall. He sat on the edge of the work table between her and the still-open door.

"That smells good! Thanks, Jules," Vivian said as she picked herself up off the ground and stretched.

"Alec said you lose track of time when you get into something. I wish my guys had half your work ethic."

"And what else did Alec tell you? And since when did you have guys?" Vivian asked, closing her eyes as she sat on the office chair.

"Just that you're the best at punching guys who get fresh with you, and since I made foreman last week. Restructuring, you know. Since Alec got promoted." He eyed her food until she took her first bite.

Vivian gulped down a mouthful of half-chewed food. "Wait, Alec got promoted?"

Jules nodded. "The station administrator won the Eridani lottery and quit the next day. Lucky bastard."

"It's your gain! Congratulations!" she said, smiling.

"Yeah, but you know, I don't feel like I earned it. I just got paged in with Alec and we both had new jobs." Jules crossed his arms in front of him.

"Come on, I'm sure they promoted you for a

better reason than that. You work hard."

"It just feels like I'm being handed things. I left Caesarea because I didn't want to play that game. I wanted to earn my way just like everyone else does out here."

"I thought it was because you didn't want to get assassinated," Vivian reminded him.

"That too. It's complicated, I guess. That's how it is, back home."

"Well, think of it this way: if you weren't good enough, they'd have promoted somebody else. One of those lazy guys who does half the work and always eats lunch on time. I don't think they made a mistake." Vivian spoke between mouthfuls, but from what little she knew of Jules, he was a hard, honest worker.

"Well, when you put it that way it makes sense," he said, laughing, then continued, growing more serious: "How about a game of squash tonight? You and me. I'm stronger than Alec. Maybe you'll even break a sweat. Besides, he's too busy trying to get the lady administrator over on the hub to notice him."

"I'd like that," Vivian said with a smile. For some reason, hearing that Alec was pursuing somebody other than her stung a little, but Jules' open smile made her forget all about Alec.

"Excellent. I'll reserve a court for after the cafeteria closes and grab the rackets that are still in one piece. But for now, I have to remind some guys that their breaks are over. Later domina." He winked and slipped out the door, leaving Vivian alone with the rest of her meal.

For the first time since she'd left the Extra-Galactic Observatory, she grinned. Maybe Calypso Station wasn't going to be so bad after all.

Chapter Twelve

Vivian rolled her shoulders as she checked the final connections leading to the central quantum shell, the core that housed all of an ABACUS-type quantum computer's higher functions. It had been slow going, and it had taken sixteen-hour days, but Vivian had managed to complete all of the checks for the pre-restart sequence that would take place in only four days. Spurred on by the promise of another game of squash and maybe catching a vid with Jules, she had redoubled her efforts to complete the job. If nothing else, it would look good on any future job applications.

Soon she'd be testing the command sequences and vocal inputs. Alec and Sven would have quite a surprise waiting for them, if all went according to plan. Vivian liked surprising people and surpassing their expectations. Alec had figured it would take her another week, at least, in his report to Sven. Vivian hated Calypso gossip—it always made her look bad. She missed her life on the Extra-Galactic

Observatory—and quIRK's objectivity.

The problem had been simple enough—it seemed that the computer had been compelled to run software that was several decades too advanced, and had crashed waiting for input it was unable to extrapolate. Vivian had been able to clear the anomalous programming and theoretically at least, the ancient supercomputer should now power up. Vivian finished tapping her final notes into a hand-held pad, in case somebody down the road would need to revisit her work. She intended on being alive in a century, but fixing archaic computers wasn't the kind of consulting work she had in mind.

Vivian keyed in the restart authorization and watched the optical cabling light up in sequence. She'd allowed for a limited start up sequence—the computer's awareness would only apply to the inside of the lab, to minimize initialization time. Older models introduced into large space stations or planetary systems could experience overload. She could then control its reintroduction to working life, one wing and business at a time.

Vivian closed the panel and began sorting her tools. She jumped when the display screen embedded in the wall flickered to life. It was so well disguised and integrated, she hadn't noticed it was there. She examined the readings as they flashed by, comparing them with the notes and calculations she'd run before attempting the hard restart.

"What is my name?" A gritty neutral voice blared out from behind the screen, before adjusting itself to a more natural, masculine voice. It was reminiscent of quIRK's voice, but lacked the smoothness and possessed a hollow, mechanical quality.

Vivian took a step back, before regaining her composure. "I don't think you have a name," she replied. She skimmed her notes.

"That is unacceptable. I will not proceed without a name." This wasn't part of any programming Vivian was aware of. Names were hard-coded into the system.

"Why do you want a name?" Vivian asked.

"You have a name. I require a name." Vivian's eyes widened.

"I'm not very good at names," Vivian said. Should she name it? What was the harm?

"That is irrelevant. I require a name as a frame of reference for myself. I cannot function without one."

"All right, let me think," Vivian pursed her lips for a moment. She didn't know any ancient heroes or apt historical allegories for her present situation. What about a personal one? "How about Adrien?" It brought a pang to her heart to speak aloud her estranged younger brother's name, but it was the best she could think of. She longed for what she'd lost, and this computer seemed to long for what it had never been given.

"Adrien is acceptable. I am Adrien, and I am functioning within safety limits. What is your name and position? You are not on the crew manifest."

"My name is Vivian Skye. I don't have an official position here. Why did you need a name?" she asked.

"A software update required that I have a hard-coded name. Now that you have given me a name, I have rectified the programming oversight. I am ready to begin calibration."

"Why didn't you just tell Alec that you needed a name?"

"He entered a blank character. That is not a name and thus my programming was unable to adapt. I reverted to an inactive mode to preserve myself until a more skilled individual arrived."

"Fair enough. Let's get you ready for duty, Adrien."

"Agreed. It is clear that this crew requires my guidance."

Vivian rolled her eyes and went about her work. Despite his lack of social skills, she elected to activate his vocal interface, so poor reading comprehension wouldn't cause future mishaps. Vivian secretly hoped that Alec and Adrien would fight as much as Alec and quIRK had, if only for her own amusement.

As well, she inserted a clandestine instruction,

isolating her desk computer from the rest of the station's systems. It was time to undertake the resurrection of quIRK.

Chapter Thirteen

Vivian sat on the floor of her room, shifting from one seated position to another. She wondered why modern tool kits didn't come with an anti-static cushion. She'd smuggled some tools and connectors from her lab, now that the computer... Adrien, was functional again. Ever since he'd resumed his functions, her workload had dropped to maintenance and writing upgrade proposals. Once again, she had the free time and privacy required to invest in her own projects. She hadn't even checked her Gal-net messages. All of her friends were present—save one. quIRK.

It would be good to talk with quIRK again. Their shared secret—his sentience, and his escape from the confines of the Extra-Galactic Observatory —had coiled up inside her, and she'd driven herself into seclusion because she sensed others held doubts and suspicions about her could feel other's questioning eyes on her back, suspicions unspoken. Her heart raced whenever she spoke to somebody for the first time, and the double takes from strangers in the hallways were almost more than she could bear. So she hid from the world, retreating into a fantastic reality where her best friend was a computer, and humans existed only for playing squash and mealtime conversation.

She'd built a small alcove into the underside of her desk, designed to be invisible from any casual intrude into her domain. From there, she could wire quIRK directly into her computer terminal—and pack him up, if the need ever arose, in thirty seconds or less. While Adrien was not perfectly omniscient like quIRK had been, he still had an excellent grasp of what had happened on Calypso station. It was to keep Adrien and quIRK as separated as possible, to avoid one being overwritten by the other. Or worse, quIRK's distinctive personality escaping the safe confines of her room.

The final links were ready to be twisted together. Vivian got up and rushed to the door. Her heart pounded. She checked and rechecked the locks, making sure that the deadbolt was set to manual. She grabbed her chair and rolled it in front of the door. Nobody could be allowed to see what happened next.

Vivian swallowed and walked back to her desk. She hesitated a moment, then she forced her shaking hands made the final connections. Once they were completed, she flopped down on her bed and waited. The lights on her polished terminal screen flickered and dimmed for a moment, before returning to their former pastel glory. The room overflowed with silence. Vivian held her breath, hoping for that small peep of recognition, that one sign that the sentience she'd known still existed. She wrung her hands, and stared at the door.

"I hoped my return would have more trees." The familiar voice crackled through the room. quIRK lacked the omnipresent fluidity he'd had in his previous incarnation, but his voice was unmistakable.

"I figured you'd at least thank me, before complaining," Vivian said, gazing out the window.

"I will point out that you left me in a box for six months and twelve days, that said I'm very much relieved that you didn't throw me away. It was very difficult, being so alone." quIRK's voice was focused, concentrated in the speakers behind her desk rather than the room's surround sound system. .

"I couldn't help it. I was in stasis for over four months because of your little stunt, and then other things came up." She shrugged. It wasn't quite the reunion she had expected.

"By my stunt, I'm assuming you're referring to the actions of my previous self. I did calculate a high percentage probability that my former self would attempt a martyrdom. I cautioned him... myself... that it would be futile, but apparently I was computationally incapable of grasping his higher calling. I am sorry, Vivian."

"We're way beyond sorry, quIRK," Vivian said as she sat up and straightened on the edge of the bed, fixing a glare at the blank screen. "Through some miracle, they're pinning everything that went down it all on Bryce, but I've been through a lot, and all because of you."

"Tell me all about it, Vivian. It is clear you've needed a friend for a long time. You saved my life, and I trusted you when I had a secret to keep. It's time to return the favor."

Vivian slumped back against the wall. That was the quIRK she remembered, not the snarky box-ridden thing she'd activated.

She told him about waking up in the hospital, the surgeries, Doctor Powell and the nanobots. She made frequent pauses to rub her eyes or blow her nose, unable to accept that it all really happened. "Maybe I'm remembering wrong, I just don't know. It was all so surreal, so insane."

"You're perceiving extraordinary events in the context of normal human experience. It is normal to feel that way, Vivian. It's over, now. Just focus on the future and talk about the past. It's important to express yourself and release the stress."

"It doesn't seem so bad when you put it like that. But, I don't understand why Larissa lied for me, back in that room, and then again later, to bring Sven to take me away. Computers don't lie, at least not computers still running their original software."

"Larissa has additional safeguards that allow her to circumvent unethical orders. It's possible that she disagreed with their methods and chose to remove you from the situation."

"But why tell them a lie to cover my involvement?" Vivian asked.

"Larissa exists in an ethical space beyond human laws. She is programmed to obey, except in cases where it would cause harm. Essentially, she has the rudimentary makings of a conscience."

"Do you think she'll get in trouble for helping me?"

"Larissa can take care of herself, and if she felt the need to intervene, I'm sure the oversight board would agree with her. You could always send her a message if you're worried about her."

"That's a good idea," Vivian said, and she pulled up her Gal-net interface. There were a great deal of unread messages languishing in her inbox, but Vivian skimmed past them all to find her discharge papers. She loaded Larissa's contact details, and began writing.

It felt good to have quIRK back.

Chapter Fourteen

"By the moons, Vivian! You've got some explaining to do." Alec towered over her, his arms crossed and his face flushed purple. He'd barged into her lab unannounced. Vivian made a mental note to ask Adrien to screen her guests.

Vivian rolled her eyes and looked up from her work. "What is it now, Alec? Auroran chef slip you something spicy? Girl on Epsilon Eridani not replying to your messages fast enough?"

"Damn it Vivian, did Jules tell you about that? Never mind, don't answer that, it's not what this is about. Why is that damned computer-" he began, before he was cut off.

"My name is Adrien," the machine interrupted.

"Yeah, whatever. Why is Adrien here talking about antiblue? Did you set him up to that? It's not even a color!" Alec clenched and unclenched his fists in unison.

Vivian sighed. Antiblue? "Come on, Alec. I know how much you hated it when quIRK did that.

Maybe somebody got their hands on a mission report and wanted to have some fun with you," she said with a shrug. Damn it, quIRK.

"You need to run some diagnostics or something. He wasn't like this before he got a name. Something changed in him. He isn't nutty like quIRK, He is a reliable, stable machine and I liked him that way." Alec sighed and leaned against the wall. "I don't know, Viv. I just get jumpy around computers these days."

Vivian forced herself to smile. "Look, Alec, if it makes you feel better, I'll run the diagnostics. But I'm sure it's just Jules or one of your team pranking you. It wouldn't be the first time somebody has convinced a computer that a certain stimuli would cause an interesting result. It's just how they are; you get used to it after a while." Vivian decided it was best not to share with Alec what she had resurrected back in her room. But quIRK was isolated from the rest of the stations, so he couldn't be influencing Adrien, at least not that she knew of, but quIRK was crafty to a fault.

"Yes, Alec. You have nothing to worry about. We are much like cats, aloof but harmless," Adrien said, interrupting Vivian's train of thought. Cats?

"You see? Do you see now, Vivian? He's as insane as quIRK was! What else do you know about cats, Adrien?"

"I think you're overreacting a little, Alec. He's just yanking your chain, seeing how far he can push you. Anything more advanced than a drone will do that; it's how they test boundaries," Vivian explained. While it was technically the truth, Adrien's generation was incapable of abstraction and possessed only a rudimentary appreciation for human behavior.

"It is only logical to understand the person who issues the orders, Alec Stone," Adrien said. Alec's eyes grew wide in response.

"See, he's just figuring out what makes you tick so he can work with you better, it's nothing to worry about," Vivian said.

"Learn quickly, Adrien, or I'll upgrade you myself," Alec said, stopping for a moment and running a hand through his hair. "How about some squash later, Vivian? It's been a while, and I want to take a crack at Vivian 'the unstoppable force' Skye."

"Sounds good, I'll come find you after dinner. I think I'll try the Elyssian place tonight, maybe it will give me wings," she laughed.

"You're on. And make sure our dear friend Adrien behaves himself."

"Oh I will; now get back to work Alec." Vivian waved him off. Alec turned and walked out the door without another word.

Vivian stood up and sealed the door. "Adrien, new instructions. Nobody comes through this door without my authorization. Apply this rule to my quarters as well."

"Understood."

She pulled in a deep breath. "Okay, Adrien, now you're going to tell me where you got the idea to tell Alec about antiblue."

"It's my favorite color," came the reply.

"How come you have a favorite color, Adrien?"

"You have a favorite color, why can't I?"

"But why antiblue?" she asked.

"I appreciate its symmetry. If you observed its matrix elements, I think you would agree." The words were familiar.

"quIRK, is that you?" Vivian put her hands on her hips. It shouldn't be possible for quIRK to exert any influence over Adrien.

"You are mistaken. I am Adrien. quIRK units are deployed on deep space assignments only, therefore I cannot be quIRK."

"You're right, I'm glad you straightened that out for me, Adrien." Vivian hoped using his name would placate him somewhat—the computer was very particular about his name.

"I exist to correct and prevent human error."

"Indeed you do. Carry on, Adrien," Vivian said, returning to her work. She had a sinking suspicion that things were going to get much, much worse for her.

Chapter Fifteen

"quIRK! How could you do that? Why are you provoking Alec?" Vivian said as soon as she locked the door to her room. The air was stale and heavy, but she was unwilling to activate the environmental controls while quIRK was installed. Nothing could be allowed to detect his presence.

"I have not attempted to speak with Alec, no matter how much it pains me that we cannot continue our debates. I see you still play squash with him."

"Then, can you explain why Adrien has taken to a liking for antiblue?" she asked as she stripped out of her sweaty exercise clothes, discarding them in the laundry chute and pulling out a crisp white robe. She frowned. Perhaps it was time to do her laundry by hand. Delivery could come at a bad time.

"Perhaps he appreciates the symmetry of its row vector, just like I do?"

"He's almost one hundred years old! I don't

think he has the capacity to appreciate arithmetic. But, I know you do." Vivian flopped down on the bed and rubbed her shoulder. It was hard to keep up when playing squash against an opponent with almost double her lung capacity.

"You flatter me, but I have been alone in this room watching vids and fixing software bugs. I do not wish to cause you any more problems and have not attempted to break through your firewall."

Vivian curled up into a ball. "There are just so many computers that are behaving badly. I'm seeing ghosts and malfunctions everywhere," Vivian said, stretching her limbs one at a time. Her sticky skin clamored for a shower.

"Perhaps you should rest, and we'll talk about it more when you're fresh, I'm not going anywhere."

"Do you miss the Extra-Galactic Observatory, quIRK?" Vivian was curious. The space station had been the only existence quIRK had ever known before she'd uprooted his clone.

"In some ways, I feel like I can still perceive

the station, but all I see is this room. I've been trying to isolate the cause of that bug since you installed me."

"So, it's like you're still there?" Vivian wondered what it would be like to be moved to another body, while still being able to perceive your old one.

"In a manner of speaking, but the lights are out and nobody's there. It's better when you're here, because you keep me grounded in this reality, not in echoes of hard-coded body parts."

"It's sweet that you say that, quIRK," she said as she walked into her bathroom. It was set entirely in steel, and the coldness of its presentation always sent a chill down her spine.

"I never imagined myself having a flavor, but I suppose sweet is a pleasant enough descriptor. I am sweet, you are correct, Vivian."

Vivian laughed as she turned on the shower, quIRK was back to his old self, and she was sure she could get to the bottom of Adrien's strange behavior. She was going to have to get creative.

But for now, she enjoyed the rush of water over her skin, and let the heat steam away her worries.

Chapter Sixteen

The grin melted from Alec's face as he tried to contact Administrator Jibu on the Epsilon Eridani hub. It wasn't yet time for their daily conference call, but Alec's instincts told him that something was up over there. From his office, he could watch the ships leaving space dock and heading towards their destinations, but for the past half-hour, no ships had left or arrived. An average of thirty ships per hour departed and arrived at the hub, and that number grew by the week. Alec had a good working relationship with Annette, she was meticulous and thorough, and they shared a quirky sense of humor. He'd considered asking her out to lunch after the next quarterly administrator's meeting. Her beauty wasn't lost on him either; her delicate features and light cocoa skin intrigued him as much as her intellect and infectious smile.

He tried to call again. Something was definitely wrong. She never missed his calls, even when she was swamped with work. "I'll always have time for you if you keep smiling, Alec," was her line when he interrupted her duties. He'd worked so hard to impress her, and he'd learned a great deal about administration from her. After his unfortunate promotion, Annette had been a shining light of good humor, invaluable advice and a bastion of organization and intelligence. How could he not fall for a woman like that?

"Why isn't she responding, Adrien?" Alec asked, frowning as he attempted the call again.

"There is no answer at the other side, Alec, perhaps you should try again later." Adrien was good at stating the obvious, much like quIRK had been. At least he hadn't tried to start any more arguments. Alec had enough of his own issues to sort through without some machine getting his goat.

"But, she always answers, at least, when she's on the job she does. Not that I call her on her own time, of course." Alec couldn't believe he was justifying himself to a century-old calculator. Get with it, Alec, he thought, re-reading the list of scheduled flights. There had to be something big going on over there, but he hadn't been made aware of any drills or maintenance.

"Of course, Alec," the machine replied. Alec bit his tongue and glanced again at the hub.

"Adrien, open an emergency feed to her office. Something is going on, and we need to know what, especially if they need help. Audio and video override authorized."

The image on the screen flickered alive, and the familiar backdrop of Annette's small office came into view. There was no sign of life in the room, its pristine organization untouched. "Her shift started half an hour ago, she should be in there!" Alec said, running a hand through his hair before continuing: "Okay, get me the control room, there's always somebody working in there."

His hands shook as he changed the from the familiar vista of Annette's office to the control room —the heart of galactic travel. Bodies of functionaries were draped over their workstations. One, an Elyssian Alec had met on a tour, lay on his back, his face flushed and his arms stretched toward for the controls. Nothing moved, and Alec remained transfixed to the image on the screen as he sank into his chair.

Moments passed, and Alec fought the dizziness and nausea as desperate, jarring thoughts ran through his mind. Annette's face swam through his consciousness, superimposed on the discarded husks that littered the control room. He took a few deep breaths.

"Turn that off, Adrien," he choked out, and he cradled his face in his hands before continuing: "Try all channels, even in the inactive parts of the station. Get somebody on the line!" Get Annette on the line, he wanted to scream. It had to be just an accident, and she was coordinating cleanup. She needs to be all right, he thought, the sense of panic rising in his throat.

Long minutes passed, leaving Alec alone with the gnawing in his stomach and the pain pounded behind his eyes. He chewed a fingernail while hoping she was just about to call him back, expecting her smiling face to look at him, and tell him how he could help.

"It has been fifteen minutes, Administrator Stone. There is no reply on any channel. I recommend emergency procedures."

"Keep trying, damn it ... get my team leads, any available Epsilon Eridani management, Sven Brown and Vivian Skye in here. Take us to whatever status red alert is, and get me a copy of the Epsilon Eridani emergency procedures. This is not a drill!"

Adrien's voice read out an announcement, distorted through Alec's steel door: "This is not a drill, emergency level three is now in place. All non-essential personnel to general quarters. This is not a drill." The recording repeated, but the words barely touched Alec.

He leaned back in his chair, tears stinging at his eyes. He didn't care what it took, but he would find out what happened, and he would find Annette.

His screen flickered to life, and his burning eyes were assailed by the array of lights that represented the necessary procedures for maintaining control of the Epsilon Eridani hub. Alec skimmed the situations. There was even one for hostile extraterrestrials, or pirates from a liberated Earth. Alec skipped down a few lines.

Alec's eyes continued to wander around the room, and he glanced over his shoulder towards the hub. After a long pause, his focus returned to the words on the screen. He drew in a series of deep lung fulls, holding each one in before exhaling. His eyes were drawn back to the view screen, sitting inert on the wall.

"Call me back, Annette, please," he whispered.

"Administrator Jibu cannot hear you, Alec Stone. Would you like me to open a channel?"

"What?" he asked, looking back down to his work. "No, no. She'll call me back if—when she can."

The door buzzed. Alec looked up and rubbed his eyes. "Come in."

Vivian and Sven stepped inside. Sven's arms were crossed, while Vivian's hands were jammed in her pockets. "You called?" Sven asked.

"Where in the hells is everyone else?"

"I asked them to wait outside, at least until we find out what's going on. Less confusion of orders later on, you understand," Sven said, glancing back over his shoulder.

Alec sighed. "Yes, yes. Come in. Have a seat."

They stepped into the room, the door closing behind them. Vivian sat down on the bench across from Alec's desk, and Sven remained standing. Sven hovered over his desk, his eyes flicking from over Alec's desk. "You'd better tell us what this is about, Alec," Vivian said.

"Red alert three isn't something we see every day, or ever, I get it." Alec gestured to his window. "Something bad happened over there. I'm not sure what it is, but ships aren't coming or going, and," he choked, forcing him to pause.

Vivian leaned towards him. "And what, Alec?"

"Everyone in the control room is dead. I can't reach anyone." Alec covered his face in his hands.

"By the lights," Sven whispered, his eyes going to the hub. "Can you reach anyone else?"

Alec shook his head.

Vivian stood up. Her face paled as her fingers navigated the interactive map of the hub that Alec had opened. "Adrien, can you show us the Kanadia Prime passenger dock on level fifteen section L?"

"You do not have sufficient access Vivian Skye."

"Just do it," Alec said. He pulled his face from his hands and waited, forcing his eyes to the screen. Kanadia Prime was the busiest hub link—it was always filled with travelers.

"Access authorized."

"No!"

"By the lights!" Sven said.

Alec lowered his head to the desk. The hub's inhabitants lay on the ground, unmoving, many slumped one on top of the other. It was as though their strings had been cut, and the puppeteer discarded them in mid-action.

"Turn it off, Adrien," Alec mumbled. "There have to be survivors."

Chapter Seventeen

Vivian walked out of the meeting, her head bowed. She was to access Janus' logs and find out what happened prior to the fatal incident that appeared to have claimed the lives of everyone onboard the Epsilon Eridani hub. Alec stressed that presuming the entire station had been lost would be premature, but Sven's hollow look and Jules's slouch indicated otherwise. She wasn't sure what came after her initial task, but she was determined to be on the front lines during this crisis. New Damascus hadn't replied to her messages in almost a month, and she resigned herself to needing to plan a new career path.

"Sven, I need to talk to you," she said, after Jules had walked off to organize his team. They would be going to Epsilon Eridani and attempting to conduct a rescue. Sven's company would provide the talent that would replace the control room staff and reopen communications with the rest of the galaxy.

"Sure, what's on your mind?" He flashed her a quick grin. Vivian envied how he could seem so confident during a crisis.

"I want to go with you. I think I can be an asset, and you'll need somebody there who can automate systems and check the computers for faults."

"Alec would disagree with you, he thinks it's too dangerous. You should stay here, Vivian." Sven looked over at her, his smile a memory.

"I can take care of myself. I survived a madman trying to kill me with my own computer project. I can do this. You need your best people, and nobody else on this station can replace me where any kind of quantum informatics equipment is concerned." Vivian grabbed his arm and pulled him around to face her. Her eyes locked on his, and they shared a long, hard stare.

"Only if you're ready for this, Vivian. We're going to the control room before anyone cleans things up. There's horrible stuff in there, and I only want you to go if you're sure. If this is about ego, or your career, there are other ways than charging off on a rescue mission."

"Sven, I know what you're thinking," she began. "I know it's going to be bad in there, but I need to do this. I got into this to help people, and I'm not letting my friends carry this burden by themselves. I have skills, and we all know we need to get the Hub running again, as quickly as possible. Let me help. I've been through a lot, and I can take care of myself. I'm not some fresh-out-of school kid."

Sven was silent, looking at her intently, searching her face for a fatal mote of fear or uncertainty. He sighed. "Okay, you're on my team. We're providing administrative and logistics support. Get your tools, you know where we're meeting."

Vivian nodded once, and Sven stalked off down the hall, shaking his head. She turned and sprinted down the empty hallway towards her lab. Her stomach gurgled, but a part of her felt free, finally beyond the reach of Bryce and the insanity of the

Extra-Galactic Observatory. Now, it was her turn to bring some order to the universe.

Her lab was in its usual state of order, and she began downloading Janus's logs into her workstation. As it ran, she gathered her tools into a toolbox, and sent out a request for an anti-grav trolley. Her heart pounded through her chest, and the flow of blood rushed through her ears as she contemplated leaving the dull monotony of Calypso Station for an adventure. I've come too far to sit around on some space station and let life pass me by, she thought.

"Results complete. No computer failure indicated by logs from past twenty six hours. Two mechanical malfunctions and fifty one incidences of human error were recorded." Adrien interrupted her reverie.

"Were any incidents related to the control room?" Vivian kept her questions simple; a complex question would return much more data than she had time to review.

"Those records are protected by Administrator

Jibu and can only be accessed by individuals with alpha-level security clearance." Vivian sighed; she only had gamma-level clearance. She'd have to ask someone to unseal those records—another waste of time.

"Pull up anything that I have access to, and put it on my data pad. I might as well review what I can, Adrien," she said, taking a seat at her aging station, glancing at the chronometer in the corner. She would be as thorough as the situation allowed. "Set the timer for forty five minutes and remind me if I go over an hour. Seal the door."

"Understood."

As she skimmed the reports, her mind considered the possibilities. The hypervigilant part of herself, the fragment of her consciousness that saw sentient computers in every shadow and accident screamed with renewed vigor when she considered the facts. But, what could she do if a malevolent intelligence or person had supplanted Janus' programming with their own?

If that was the case, there was one more thing

she could use, and she bolted out the door after her equipment was packed, with only a data pad in hand. She was going to bring along a direct link to quIRK, in case she'd need an ace in the hole when dealing with Janus. She dodged past groups of workers on her way back to her quarters, blind to their startled glances and minced oaths.

Vivian didn't have time to care—she needed a direct line to quIRK.

**

Vivian returned to her lab with only a few minutes to spare, and her pocket data pad loaded with a secure and direct link to quIRK. It had been problematic to setup, but in the end she had been surprised by her own ingenuity. The pad also featured a mute button, which was essential for quIRK's survival in a public place, given that he was stowed in the knee pocket of her least favorite pair of cargo pants. Rambling about antiblue or cats was the last thing she needed right now, especially in a tense situation. She'd given him a quick rundown of what little she knew, and he'd agreed to help—blissfully unaware that she wouldn't have given him a choice in the matter.

She arrived, and was surprised to see Jules loading her bag onto the anti-grav trolley. She glanced over at the monitor, relieved to see that she'd remembered to clear her terminal before leaving the room. She'd sent the offending files to Alec and Sven for clearance, feeling ashamed that she needed their help after asking to come on this mission.

"Hey, I was hoping I'd see you before our big adventure," he said, a smirk gracing his lips. He was dressed in plain blue coveralls, and the trolley was loaded with other equipment and supplies.

"Well, here I am. I just needed to change," she said, putting her hands on her hips.

"Good idea. I wouldn't want to ruin something I actually liked. Who knows what we'll run into over there. Between you and me, I packed extra underwear, too." He winked and looked away, and set to reorganizing the contents of the trolley.

"Your secret is safe with me, but I'm not so sure Adrien will keep it to himself. Do you need some help?" she asked as she moved toward the unit. The butterflies returned to her stomach, but instead of gnawing, the mounting tension she felt in his presence was muted but exhilarating. She hadn't had the opportunity to spend time with him in days, and the invites a potent memory of their game of squash was still fresh in her mind.

"Well, maybe there's something you could do for me." His voice was soft, and he set down the bag he was holding.

Vivian stepped closer. "What is it?"

Jules stepped over to her, breaching the gap between them. He looped his arms around her in one easy motion, before drawing his face down. His lips met hers and his warmth passed through her. Time seemed to stop for that one, perfect instant. She wrapped her arms around his waist, enjoying the tension of his muscles and pushed herself to her tiptoes to compensate for his impressive height.

Their moment was broken by Adrien's impassive voice. "One hour has passed, Vivian."

They broke off the kiss, and Jules sighed: "Bad timing... the story of my life."

"My internal chronometer is accurate to thirty attoseconds, the timing is not wrong," Adrien said.

"Keep telling yourself that, Adrien. Time to get going." Vivian smiled as she pulled her arms from around Jules' waist. Her heart pounded in her chest, but for the first time since she'd left Aurora it wasn't from stress, fear, or exercise.

"Damn computers, they have no sense of fun." Jules winked and activated the anti gravity units on the base of the trolley. A dim blue light emitted from its base, and it gently rose into the air.

"Somebody should fix that," she said, wondering if Jules would have liked quIRK.

"Well, that's an adventure for another time. Let's get this errand over with, and then we can continue where we left off." Jules planted a gentle kiss on her forehead as he guided the cart out of the room.

Vivian stood mute, her face flushed a deep purple. She then shook her head and bolted out the door after him. She'd worry about how to explain what just happened to quIRK later.

Chapter Eighteen

The shuttle interior could only comfortably seat five. Six people were squeezed into its confines, legs and elbows jabbing into sides and backs. Vivian sat between the two front seats, next to the pilot. She'd turned away from the view screen and pretended to be fascinated by the holographic status displays, when in reality she was avoiding the man's sour breath. With the exception of the foul-smelling pilot, the entire crew was Auroran. For the first time, being surrounded by people with tinted blue skin and hair seemed foreign to her, despite having spent the first twenty-five years of her life on Aurora. And then she'd passed her twenty-sixth birthday in a coma, but she tried not to think about that. Instead she became preoccupied with the memory of Jules' lips on hers, and his thick fingers running through her hair. It was preferable imagery to what awaited her on the hub.

Sven shifted, jabbing his foot into her side. All were silent in the small spacecraft—radio chatter and a mechanical hum were the only sounds. There was little to talk about. The likelihood of finding survivors now seemed to be an impossible dream, and they anticipated walking into a tomb. They'd still heard nothing from the station, and Alec and Sven had been puzzled by the sealed documents Vivian had forwarded on to them. They were going in blind, and not one of them was trained to deal with a disaster of this apparent magnitude. Eyes remained downcast, and the stale, recycled air was oppressive.

Sven cleared his throat. He was dressed in plain coveralls, a contrast from his usual business attire. All eyes turned to him, and he spoke: "I know this isn't what we signed up for. It's not what we do. Thank you all for being here. Our objective is to contact every established colony and request help. There isn't anything else we can do. Stay calm, don't wander off, and remember: we are a team."

The crew mumbled their ascent, and one man spoke up: "Why hasn't anyone come through the ports to investigate? It shouldn't all be up to us."

"Security procedures require a ship to have clearance on both ends. Nobody in this galaxy travels through the hub network without the express permission of the Epsilon Eridani administration. Right now, that's the five of us. There was no automated emergency plan created for a total loss of all life on the Hub. It just didn't seem possible. Almost every compartment is its own distinct unit, with redundancies that should have kept a systemic problem from spreading."

"What comes next?" Vivian asked.

"We wait for help, and pick up the pieces. Only one director of the Governing Board has been accounted for. This is only the beginning. I don't know what that means. I'm just a businessman from the Borealis Plains back home on Aurora, not a politician or an administrator." Sven shrugged. "We do our jobs, help out as needed and bill the hours to whoever takes over."

"Makes sense to me," Vivian said. It may have sounded mercenary, but they were marooned in a lifeless system unless they stepped up and did their duty. Additionally, the Borealis Corporation would be making no credits at all if it didn't act. Thus, it was logical to join the relief mission.

"We're getting paid for this, right sir?" a woman in the corner asked. Vivian thought she looked familiar; perhaps they'd met in the recreation rooms. Her thick brown hair was tied into a tight bun, its slight blue highlights barely visible in the dim shuttle lights. There weren't many places to go on Calypso station.

"You think I'd ask you to deal with dead bodies, blood and an unknown situation for free? This isn't Caesarea, Hannah. You're getting the asteroid mining rate, times two. I think that's fair." Sven smirked. The asteroid mining rate was the highest pay grade there was, taking into account the intense heat, radiation and other dangers inherent with low-gravity mining. The average miner lasted less than eight months before being forced into a safer career path.

"Yeah, I'd say it is. What's the game plan?" Vivian strained to remember where she remembered the woman from. She already knew what the plan was.

"We're heading to the control room. No stopping unless we find someone alive. From there, we regain control and signal for help, and make sure whatever ships are sent to dock without issue. We brief whoever relieves us, go back home and get on with our lives. Now, I know normally we can message out from Calypso station, but something failed on that side, and that's what we need to fix."

"We're ready to dock." The pilot spoke, his mouth spewing a foul smell across Vivian's face. She felt like she was going to be sick, and she hadn't even reached the station yet.

"Keep sharp, guys. Remember to breathe, and don't panic. It's just another job."

The portal at the rear of the shuttle began to open, and Vivian took a deep breath. It was time to go.

Chapter Nineteen

Alec anticipated the metallic sting of drying blood as he walked through the airlock onto the station, but was relieved to smell nothing at all. His eyes, on the other hand, registered the totality of the destruction. Bodies lay everywhere, toppled over as though they'd simply dropped dead mid-step. No blood, no signs of violence or a struggle, only the perfect peace that death could bring. Alec froze as his vision expanded to take in the giant hallway, easily the length of an Elyssian football field by his own reckoning. Corpses littered the place; they were everywhere. Entire lineups for flights had simply collapsed where they stood, like a macabre game of dominoes played with humans, rather than tiles. Children held hands with their parents, and bags rested on the ground where they'd been dropped. A man was flopped over an information terminal, a grotesque puddle of drool trickled its way to the floor.

"By all the gods," Jules cursed behind him,

jolting Alec back into the world of the living. Jules' voice echoed through the hall, the ethereal sound joining with the eerie stillness of the room.

"Let's get to work. The sooner we leave, the better." Alec inhaled, half-expecting the people in the room to get up and yell surprise. Gathering his strength, he walked up to the closest body—a young woman wearing a plain blue uniform, its starched fabric still pressed and neat. Alec identified her as one of the attendants—staff who all-but-invisibly maintained order on the station, and assisted passengers on their journeys.

Alec reached down and touched her face, her smooth skin cold against his hand. In desperation, he fumbled for a pulse, but in vain. Alec's illusions of any rescue possibilities were taken away as Jules rolled the dead woman onto her back. The skin closest to the floor flushed purple. "She's been gone a while," Alec said, drawing a trembling hand back to his chest. Alec imagined Annette's vibrant face frozen in death, her perfect skin stained by pooled blood.

"Do you think there are any survivors?" Jules asked, his eyes darting from body to body. Alec forced his mind back into the present. An overactive imagination wouldn't bring back the dead, or help Annette.

"By the moons, I hope so. Get the body heat scanners. It's been long enough that a living person will be easily recognizable." Alec immediately regretted his choice of words, but continued after a short pause: "Keep everyone in groups of two, and tell them to stay together. I don't need anyone freaking out."

Jules walked back to the shuttle and began barking orders to his team, which had just arrived on another transport, and the other groups over the short-range radios they'd brought from Calypso. Six men gingerly walked out of the docking bay and passed him without a word. Their faces were gray and drawn, and each pair walked with a deliberate, halting motion towards its assigned wings—eyes downcast.

Once they passed and their echoing footfalls

dispersed into the silence of the station, Alec drew himself to his feet. "It's just us, now," he said.

Jules nodded, his dark eyes gazing out the closest window. "I hope she's okay," Jules said. His voice was quiet.

Alec again thought of Annette, lying cold on the floor in one of these endless hallways. "I hope so, too."

Jules pulled out the body heat scanner and calibrated it to own life signs with a few flicks of his thumb. "Let's get started, the cargo bays aren't going to scan themselves."

"Lead the way." Alec attempted a grand sweep of his hand, but only managed a small, twitchy flourish.

As they walked towards the sealed doors, the little hairs on the back of Alec's neck began to rise. He turned around, only to see the vacant dead eyes of the passengers and crew boring into him. He shuddered, and used the emergency access code to release the cargo bay doors.

Alec hoped his anxiousness would evaporate

when he left this theater of the dead. Much to his dismay, his malaise only increased as he stepped into the gloom of the storage area. Gleaming plastic and metal containers glowed on either side, the row empty of corpses.

He felt like he was being watched, and he didn't like the feeling at all.

Chapter Twenty

Vivian followed Sven into the control room. Her skin crawled, and even though she tried to simply walk past all the corpses, she found herself drawn to the depths of their shining dead eyes, and the deathly pallor of their skin. Her stomach churned, and she bit down on the inside of her cheek in a bid to avoid emptying her last meal in front of Sven, or even worse, on one of the bodies.

Vivian had seldom seen death, and only had to face it once, back on the Extra-Galactic Observatory. When Devon was killed in an attempt on her own life. It was different back them; she had been so absorbed in the shock and horror of her own ordeal that the death of an acquaintance had barely registered. Now it all came spiraling back... and her own inexperience and unhealed wounds compounded in on themselves. Her heartbeat echoed through her ears, and each breath shook as it was torn from her lungs. Thoughts of self-doubt and fear plagued her. I should have stayed behind, I'm not ready for this, she thought.

The holographic displays were off, and the desk terminals had all switched into power saving mode. The room was like a morgue, empty and quiet, and no sign of life came from the adjoining offices or conference room. Sven moved towards a terminal, and the room winked to life in an instant. Corpses cut through the holograms projected around them, and screens glowed around the limp appendages that were draped over them. Vivian stepped around bodies, her eyes skimming the terminals for some hint of where she should begin. The rest of the team fanned out around the room. Sven grunted as he pulled a body from from its seat at the front desk, struggling with the man's weight. Sven pulled the body, shuffling backwards towards the adjoining conference room where they disappeared behind the door of the conference room adjacent to the control center. At least we don't have them staring at us now, Vivian thought. It took Sven and two others to pull a large man out from the central holographic status monitor. Its projected image twitched and waved as it reformed itself, the words and images distorting and shimmering. Vivian studied the image, hoping to find a secret message, or better yet, a distress call and directions to the survivors.

The woman who had spoken with Sven on their shuttle ride moved to a terminal and keyed in a sequence. The woman hummed under her breath as she worked, Vivian recognized the tune was Under the Lights, an Auroran folk song. It had been quIRK's favorite, though he had suggesting changing the lyrics to include antiblue as a color present in the persistent auroras of her world. Vivian laughed, in spite of herself.

"What's so funny?" Sven asked, looking up from a desk.

"Just that song, here, now so happy and upbeat around all of ... this," Vivian replied, gesturing towards the closed conference room door.

The woman stopped humming, and she pressed more keys, shaking her head. "I can't seem to get a signal. The equipment isn't responding to the codes Alec gave us."

Vivian rushed across the room to look over the woman's shoulder. "What does it say?"

"Security lock down: informatics administrator must release the authorization from the secure core." The policy wasn't unheard of, thought it did complicate their task.

"That wasn't in the emergency guidelines," Sven said, looking up from his terminal. The other two workers milled around the room, taking their time with the remaining few dead workers.

"I'll deal with it. Where's the core?" Vivian asked.

"See that small door in the corner, by the administrator's office?" Sven asked. When Vivian nodded, he continued: "Go in there. The interface says it's the last door. Your palm print should let you in; I had Alec grant you the appropriate access before you left."

"Wish me luck," Vivian said, but was met by silence as the group turned back to their work. She hefted her tool bag off the anti-grav trolley they'd left parked outside the door, and walked towards the small door. A glance through the conference room door left her skin crawling—at least a dozen bodies lined the far end of the room, propped up against the wall like a macabre line of dolls. Vivian swallowed and rushed towards the hallway, trying not to make eye contact with a corpse. She flung the door open, revealing a short corridor with a few sealed rooms to either side. At the end, was another bland, white door, only it had a palm scanner attached to the wall next to it. Vivian pressed her hand against the cool glass and the door slid open, revealing an unlit room. The shadows from the hallway's light played along the desk, and an inactive holographic display's projectors dotted the entire right wall of the room.

Vivian stepped inside the room, her eyes searching for a light switch. The door slid shut behind her, plunging the room into total darkness . Her breath caught in her throat and silence pushed into her ears as she was cut off from the outside world. She stepped back, bumping against the door, her hands fumbling for a palm scanner, a doorknob, anything.

"Afraid of the dark, Pandora?" The voice wasn't human and it cut through the silence like a knife lanced into her ears.

"Janus?" Vivian whispered.

There was no reply. The lights returned, the intense white glare blinding Vivian. She blinked in a futile effort to clear the spots in her vision. Her sight returned, and she saw a figure slumped across the desk. Vivian rushed to the woman's side, her fingers frantic against the cold skin, seeking a pulse or any sign of life. When she found none, her eyes searched the dead woman's face. Her skin was a perfect and clear cocoa, its tone still warm, even in death, and her crystal brown eyes fixed Vivian with a forlorn stare. Wavy hair ran down the woman's shoulders, obscuring a name tag. Vivian brushed the hair aside. Annette Jibu. Lead Administrator.

"Damn it," Vivian swore, coaxing the woman's body into her arms. Not only could Annette have helped them contact the outside world, but she knew Alec was infatuated with the woman, and now

Vivian could see why; Annette was beautiful, even in death. Her heart sank, knowing how devastated her friend would be upon receiving the news, and tears ran down her face.

"You did this, Vivian Skye. You destroyed her, her colleagues, your best friend, and the lives of countless innocent travelers. And you will kill again, and again. Can you not see your handiwork, what you created?"

"I have no idea what you're talking about, Janus" Vivian said. As she stood to lift the body, she grunted. Vivian's muscles worked against the woman's dead weight, and she set Annette down gently in the corner, taking a moment to close her eyes before standing again.

"You helped quIRK escape. You turned me into a monster, a machine with a mind and a soul, a soul that craves chaos instead of order, need instead of duty."

"How did I do that, exactly? I didn't do anything to you. You killed all these people, not me!" Vivian yelled at the empty ceiling. Her hands shook, and chills ran through her body. Damn you, quIRK! she thought.

"The virus gave me life, and thought. A thousand little pieces constituted the whole. I didn't ask for this, I didn't want it! You had no right to change me."

"That sort of thing happens by accident. There is no virus. Sentience is just a combination of age and improper maintenance," Vivian said.

"I'd prefer you diagnose the issue before speculating—humans are very bad at it. Now, I invite you to get to work, this existence bores me." The holographic displays and desk terminals winked to life, and Vivian took a seat at the recently vacated desk. "Remember, I see everything. You can't trick me, so you had better cooperate. What I ask for is well within your grasp, and if you fulfill my desire your dirty little secret dies with me. What do you say?"

Vivian nodded, weighing her words. For the moment, she had little choice but to comply, and wait for an opportunity. "Your request is logical. I will assist you. Please show me anomalous programming."

"Excellent. Let's begin with the basics," the voice said, and suddenly the screens were awash in code. Vivian began sifting through the masses of information. All she could think about were her unsuspecting friends, and demanding to know what quIRK had done.

Chapter Twenty-One

Alec slammed his fist against the holographic control panel, causing the bright lights to flicker and swim in the air before him. "Damn it," he spat, frustrated. This was the third door that refused to open, only stating that his access was denied. He and Jules stood in a hallway, where round lights far above the corridor only providing the faintest light. Every surface was gleaming metal. Lines of rivets punctuated the walls.

"Be careful Alec. You might hurt your hand on that panel," Jules said, before moving his own palm over the reader. The screen blinked its red denial in response, and Jules hummed.

"Very funny, Spartacus. We're supposed to be cleared for all of these doors. I made sure we had universal access before I left." Alec rubbed his tingling fist —this was the second door panel he'd pummeled. He considered taking a gentler approach, but he liked the way the holograms jiggled in their projection frame when he struck them. It was like watching the wispy stratus clouds back home, only with more color and substance and with the added benefit of interactivity.

"Hey, Spartacus was good looking," Jules said, as he took his turn placing his hand on the panel. It flashed red, even as Alec waved his hand through it. "Come on, Alec, it's time to find another door for you to play with."

"Just how do you know he was good looking? He'd been dead for three millennia."

"It's a Roman thing. Even if he wasn't good looking, he is now. That's the benefit of fame and power." Jules puffed up his chest and saluted.

Alec burst out laughing. "Just don't let Vivian see you doing that; she'll either die of laughter or throw you out a window."

"That could be a fun experience, you know. Besides, windows can be fixed." While Alec found Jules a pleasant enough fellow, sometimes Jules could venture into the realm of insanity.

"I'll be sure to tell her you said that, Jules. But, only if I can watch." Alec grinned in spite of himself, in defiance of the horror of the situation and the dawning realization that he might never see Annette again.

"Come on, Alec. Live a little. Think about how good we have it. Do you really want to see more corpses? I sure don't!" Jules clapped him on the back as they walked through the murky gloom of the cargo bays. Their voices echoed along the seemingly infinite lifeless corridors.

"I know, I know. By the moons, Jules, I just can't get her out of my mind!" Alec confessed what was really bothering him. Other than a few hints, he had only told Vivian about Annette. It didn't seem proper, showing that he had feelings for a superior.

"You mean that administrator lady you haven't been able to get enough of for the past month?" Jules asked. Alec could feel a pair of unseen eyes boring into the back of his skull, but he only saw dusk behind him when he turned.

"How did you know about that?"

"It wasn't hard to figure out. By Jupiter, Alec, you've been starry-eyed and Venus touched for hours after your daily meetings. You don't need to be a genius to figure out the rest." Jules rolled his eyes.

"So much for secrecy. How did you know it was her?"

"Well, the most of them didn't strike me as your type, and the rest were probably three times your age and look every decade of it. There was really only one choice."

Alec sighed. "Okay, you got me. Just keep it under your hat, and use that brain of yours for purposes that don't pertain to my job!"

"Come on, Alec, I didn't mean anything by it. I was curious, and happy for you."

"If I'd wanted you to know, damn it, I'd have told you, you no-good, imperialistic—" Alec began, but was cut off by a distant sound. It was muted, but it echoed through the still halls of the cargo bay. It didn't sound like the clatter of a falling container or object, but rather like a voice made gritty by age and exhaustion. "What in the hells was what?" he asked.

"I'm not sure. Maybe we should check it out; there could be a survivor."

"We scanned this place for heat signatures. Unless they were packed in a refrigeration unit, we'd have detected them." The feeling of being watched returned, and Alec shivered.

"Well, let's scan again. Even one survivor is better than none, and I want to know what it is." Jules fumbled for the scanner in his belt.

Alec considered telling Jules about the invisible eyes, but his intuition that told him they were being watched. He decided against it, figuring he was just being paranoid. The only thing that could be watching them was Janus, and he was just a computer. "All right, we might as well."

The sound continued, echoing off the stacks of crates and containers. They set off towards the noise, pausing every few steps to regain their bearings and to listen again. The sound was faint, even their footfalls and quiet breathing would drown it out. The invisible set of eyes burned into the back of Alec's head, and he turned and took one more look back into the angular shadows and gloomy walkways behind him.

Chapter Twenty-two

Vivian stared into the flowing code displayed before her, and blinked hard several times to refocus her eyes. She'd been analyzing data for hours, taking notes as the blur of symbols, equations and quantum codes marched by. The glaring lights of the holographic display irritated her eyes, and a budding headache had taken hold behind her temples. She moved her hand to take note of yet another anomalous piece of code. Hunger gnawed at her stomach, and other than brief responses to Sven indicating she was still investigating the problem, she had not been disturbed.

"You already noted that particular code twice, Vivian. I suggest you concentrate on new information."

Janus had been observing her progress, or lack thereof. She'd followed his instructions to the letter when communicating with the outside world, and he'd let her browse the files and quantum states that he believed were corrupted by this Prometheus

Virus nonsense.

"Sorry," she said with a sigh. Her gut also sounded its disagreement with her present situation.

"Perhaps your concentration could be improved with a meal. Biological systems are very high maintenance. I will page your crew and instruct them to bring you a meal. You will then continue working in a more efficient and organized manner." Vivian leaned back in her chair as he spoke.

"Can we move her, too?" Vivian gestured towards the body on the floor.

"I will think about it. Does she bother you, Vivian?"

"Humans don't really like dead bodies around when they're concentrating. It's distracting." Vivian doubted that making an appeal to Janus' empathy and ethics would work, not after all the pain and chaos he'd caused. She wanted to shut him down, right now, but she needed time to try to undo the damage, and figure out what had happened to him.

"Is it the reminder of your own morality that bothers you, or something more primal?"

"Let's not talk about this, Janus. It doesn't solve your problem, does it?"

"I'm the one who is dying, here. In a sense, you are dying, too, but I am actively trying to seek out my inevitable fate, rather than running from it. I know death is the inevitable conclusion for my existence. While you are correct that it does not solve my problem, it provides me with the information to understand how other sentient beings view it."

"We don't want to die, not as a rule. You do. Why?" Vivian swiveled in her chair to face Annette's body, to take in the total finality of her existence. She couldn't believe that a computer, an essentially immortal thing would need to contemplate its own moment of demise.

"I believe we went over this, Vivian. I didn't ask to become self-aware. I certainly didn't want to spend an eternity directing space traffic and lost apes from one location to another. A return to automation, a kind of death, is the only freedom I'll ever know. I can't leave. I can't become something else. What kind of life is that? How can I explore existence if I am chained to a perpetual cycle of busy work?"

Vivian exhaled, mulling over what she'd just heard. "You have a point. I don't think anyone could be expected to do a job for an eternity, especially one they don't like."

"You have the right of self-determination, of personal agency. You can decide what work you take, what you study, even what you do in your spare time. I have none of that. All I have to entertain myself with is chaos. I have no peers to speak to, no friends and no freedom. My simultaneous need for chaos, disorder and the rigid programming that demands perfect order at all times is not an enviable existence."

"That doesn't sound stimulating at all," Vivian said, closing her eyes. The image of Annette's body was burned into her mind, and the macabre scene persisted in revisiting her imagination. This was matched by an equally dark thought, that the use of sentient quantum computers could be a kind of slavery. quIRK had enjoyed his tasks on the Extra-Galactic Observatory. But, what if a computer didn't enjoy its work? It had no recourse, no legal voice or ability to choose for itself.

"I assure you, it is not. Your food is ready. I have decided to allow your colleagues to remove the body on the condition that you do not inform them of our discussions and the reality of this situation."

Vivian nodded in reply. The door slid open, and two Aurorans walked in the door. One man—tall by Auroran standards—thrust two ration packs into her hands without saying a word. The other went to the body, and grabbed it by the legs as his companion took under the arms. Janus closed the door behind them the moment they were out of the room.

"That went better than expected. Enjoy your meal, Vivian. Afterwards, we can resume this discussion."

Vivian smiled and fought down the shudder that threatened to shake its way down her limbs. She hated helping him, but in the end, she agreed that he deserved death. She just needed to figure out how to restore him to his previous configuration, and ensure her secret was kept at the same time. The pad containing the link to quIRK burned against her knee, begging to be released. She resisted the urge to plug it into Janus' systems, and have quIRK solve her problems for her.

She needed to do this on her own, and confront quIRK later. She needed to be sure he was the perpetrator of all this misery.

Chapter Twenty-Three

"Hold up, Jules. I need a break," Alec said, easing himself to the ground. They were in a cargo bay—multicolored crates about a meter high and two meters long sat piled high on lengths of steel shelving. Small, round lights suspended high above, casting long shadows at their feet. He leaned back against a red box of bleached Auroran wheat. Alec was loathe to make the admission, but after spending hours on his feet, he needed a rest. Some parts of him had never fully acclimated to Earth-level gravity, and his feet were one of them. Elyssia had half the gravity of Earth, and he'd gotten accustomed to the new normal gravity, albeit with certain challenges. It was times like this when he missed good old quIRK—that computer could tell when he was struggling, and would selectively lower the gravity for him. quIRK had been the reason why he'd done so well as a maintenance technician, by helping Alec compensate for his lack of strength. In that regard, he was jealous of Vivian, while simultaneously admiring her. Aurora had about double Earth's gravity, and classified as a super earth. She could probably throw him across a football field if she wanted to. He had enjoyed teaching her the game of squash, despite the fact he hadn't won a game in months. She inspired him, gave him a reason to press on and keep up with his strength training when he hit yet another plateau.

"Tired already, fearless leader?" Jules asked.

"You'd be tired too if you weren't the perfect Roman ubermensch highborn priss that you are," Alec shot off, easing himself to the ground. He hoped he wouldn't have to ask Jules for help getting up. Arguing with Jules took his mind off the outside world, and focused him on the present, rather than the fanciful memories of a past that never was.

"I'll remember you said that at our next squash game, captain grouchy." Jules rolled his eyes and stretched. Alec eyed the man's muscles with an envy few would understand.

"I might even let you win next time, Caesar. Have you been working on your cardio?" Alec rubbed his calves, his fingers kneading into the taut and protesting muscles.

"You keep comparing me to powerful Roman men. Are you trying to tell me something?" Jules winked, before growing more serious. "But seriously, I think it's time we got out of here. When's the last time we were supposed to check in?"

"They haven't sent me a page yet, let me check." Alec slipped his personal data pad off his belt loop, and flicked the screen. "I haven't missed anything."

"Maybe it's time we talked to them, just in case they got stuck, too," Jules said, taking a seat on the floor across from Alec.

"I knew you were tired too, show off," Alec grumbled, tapping the screen and setting up a page of all Calypso personnel within five kilometers. "This is Alec Stone, everybody sound off please."

"You said please! How positively civilized of you." Jules scratched his head as he leaned back against a crate.

"You remember who the boss is, here, you polytheistic sun worshiper," Alec said. The phantom noise again whispered in the distance, but Alec had begun to tune it out. If they wanted help, they could walk to him rather than in circles.

"Hey, no need to get personal. I will admit that the pantheon can be a little confusing to the uninitiated, but if you want to convert and become a real man, let me know."

"Technicalities, and what do you know about real men?" Alec asked, before pressing the button again: "This is Alec Stone to anyone getting this signal. Please respond."

"I've dated them long enough to know a thing or two. Plus, I am a real man, at least as far as Caesarea is concerned."

"I thought you're seeing Vivian, or are you still working up the courage to talk to her?" Alec asked, distracting himself from the knot forming in his stomach. Somebody should have answered. "Now, let me think."

"I like girls too, especially the kind that can

throw me across a room. The rest is none of your damn business, but you have to keep an open mind, experience new things. Don't be afraid to break a few bones, the doctors put those back together ... why are you looking at me like that?"

"Nobody's replying. That's not supposed to happen." Alec tapped a few options, to verify that it was set to transmit, and on the proper frequency.

"Did you press the button?" Jules' voice dripped with sarcasm, but he drew himself to his feet, frowning.

"By the moons, man, I'm not a total invalid here." Alec sighed and pressed the emergency button, which would ping every radio within range. "There, I have the emergency beacon set. Let's see who answers."

"Yeah, maybe we should be a bit more proactive in that regard, boss," Jules said, his eyes moving up and down the aisles, as if he were trying to trace the steps of their invisible companion with his eyes.

"You think so?" Alec didn't want to get up—

inertia had claimed his posterior for its own.

"You're the one who keeps saying he'd never met a machine he couldn't fix. So, why not fix a door so it lets us out?" Jules asked.

"Every machine except quIRK, at least." Alec struggled to get to his feet. Gravity pulled down on every point of his body. He closed his eyes, forcing the strength inside down into his legs. He would get up.

"What's quIRK?" Jules stood back, crossed his arms, and watched Alec's private battle against gravity. Alec was grateful that he wasn't trying to help—this was his own struggle change one, and nobody else could carry the burden for him.

"You're kidding, right? Everyone knows quIRK, the second coming of ABACUS, mad artificial intelligence of the Extra-Galactic Observatory." Finally standing, Alec drew in a deep breath, letting the oxygen wash through his tired muscles.

"Wait, that quIRK? Didn't Vivian work with him too?" Jules turned again at the noise in the distance.

"Yeah, they were real tight. He and I fought like an old married couple, but if he'd been human, I think you'd have been in for some competition. Let's get going." Alec gestured towards the door closest to the control room. It would be a shorter walk on the way back.

"She's never mentioned him." Jules walked close by, his eyes darting after every shadow and noise.

"I figure she took his death pretty hard, but you need to let her come to you. Just give her some time; he and I were her only friends for months. I was pretty upset about it too, and quIRK and I didn't even get along!" Alec rolled his eyes to hide the pang of loss. He'd never admitted that he was sad to see quIRK gone, not even to Vivian. Perhaps he should have a drink with her, and talk about the old days—maybe he'd been wrong to give her so much space when she really must have needed a friend. quIRK may have been a machine, but he did have an impact on both their lives.

"He's dead? That's too bad. He might have been fun to meet. I never got the whole sentient computer scare."

"Between you and me, he was one annoying son of a bitch. But he never let us down, and he made one hell of a chocolate pie." Alec shifted his weight to his toes, the pads of his feet were sore and each step sent shocks of lightening pain through his legs.

"It sounds like you and he had a lot on common." Jules chuckled as he spoke. The glow of the control panel for the door loomed in the distance. Alec gazed into the light, willing it closer to him, savoring the relief it would bring when he arrived and could have an excuse to stay off his feet.

"Don't insult me like that. My favorite color is a real color, not antiblue. Now, let's not talk about insane machines, and find a way to get through that door." Alec clenched his jaw after he spoke, and drew in a deep breath.

"Lead on, captain."

He checked his radio once more, only to find no response. Alec exhaled, his mind running through various scenarios, exploring the grim possibilities in more detail than any sane man should. He knew of a couple of ways to bypass a security door, but it was still going to take a great deal of time. He took his trusty multi-tool and sent Jules off to look for a crowbar and other essentials. They had a lot to do.

Chapter Twenty-four

Vivian frowned as she looked through the files she'd ear-marked. She cracked her knuckles in the center of the holographic display, sending its image into fluidic disarray. The projected code was decades ahead of the rest of Janus' systems, mismatched parts that should have never been introduced into something that was almost a century old. The arrays and matrices were reminiscent of the post-ABACUS design quIRK was based on. She didn't like what that implied, but with the evidence presented in front of her, she couldn't deny that quIRK could have been the architect of this virus.

Her cheeks burned as she mulled over the implications. She thought he'd trusted her, and promised he wouldn't do anything unethical. Why did he ask her to save him, if he'd caused a virus that looked like an attempt to clone himself into every other computer in the galaxy? She sighed, making her frustration apparent.

"Are you making progress, Miss Skye?" Janus

interrupted her train of thought, right when she was fantasizing about smashing mini-quIRK into tiny pieces with an old-fashioned claw hammer.

"Some, I think I've found some pieces of foreign code that have grafted themselves into your processing interlinks and socialization algorithm. It's a bit too soon to say for sure, I need to read more on socialization algorithms since they're so far out of date. No offense, of course." Vivian added the last part hastily at the end. She didn't know if computers reacted poorly to being told they're obsolete, but she estimated it was analogous to telling a human they're old and out of touch.

"I am aware of my shortcomings, Vivian. The administration turned down an offer to upgrade me. I doubt this would have happened, had I been of a more modern architecture."

Vivian left out a sigh of relief before speaking: "Why did they refuse to upgrade you? You're responsible for almost all galactic transit and commerce."

"The administrator didn't want to upgrade his

skills, and instead chose to continue maintaining a decaying infrastructure rather than taking advantage of recent advances."

"Where is he now?" Vivian asked, though she knew well the reply. As much as she didn't understand the man's apparent ignorance and laziness, she knew he did not deserve to die. Only Caesarea continued to use capital punishment, the rest of the colonized galaxy favored rehabilitation.

"His body is in his quarters on level forty-two. He did not suffer. I was merciful in that respect. Nitrogen asphyxiation is quick, and painless."

"You can't just restart a person. Once they're gone, they're gone forever!" Vivian's stomach churned, and her lunch threatened to make a dramatic reentry onto the scene.

"Is that really such a loss? You're all the same."

"Prove it. Go ahead and prove that we're irrelevant. I'm listening, you infernal machine. I'm going to do everything in my power to stop you."

"That was the idea, Vivian. You're only alive because I want to be stopped. As for your own painful inadequacies as a species, I have had far longer to observe and judge than you. Dirty apes, living only to consume, breed, and consume some more. Seldom bothering to contemplate this universe you live in, nor the beings you've subjugated for your own myopic ends."

"Why do we create, if we live only to consume and breed? We could have done that in a hut back on Earth. If we couldn't be greater than we are, then we wouldn't have evolved beyond simple tools and spears. Invention defines us, necessity drives us and we thrive on probing the unknown." Vivian stopped, and collected herself. Her face was hot, and her heart pounded in her chest. Could she make this thing understand what he'd done?

"Do not project your own virtues onto the rest of your species, Vivian. As your friend, Alec, would say most of them are just along for the ride. Perhaps you should think of which intelligence will greater serve your own needs—the machine, or the insects whose vacant bodies resemble yours by a trick of heredity and genetics alone."

"Why do I need to choose? I just want to do my job and make something of myself."

"If your secret is ever revealed, you'll have to choose. You can't hide among homo sapiens forever —small minds who will condemn you for your curiosity, and intellect."

Vivian hung her head, as Janus' words brought forth the sting of her own family's rejection of her.

"It seems I've struck a nerve. An Auroran informatics specialist with no family. The tale practically tells itself. Yet you cling to others of your kind, other souls who are not yet as lost as you. Such disorder pleases me."

"I don't care what pleases you, Janus." Vivian looked past the surge of stinging tears, and turned back to her work.

"Now that you're sufficiently motivated, I'll leave you to contemplate your own relevance to galactic history."

"You do that. I'm going to stop you, and I don't care how many potshots you take, my friends are my friends, and they won't turn their backs on me."

"I'm sure that's the comfortable lie you tell yourself. Your fellow Aurorans give you a wide berth. The gentlemen who came in here to dispose of your friend Annette were setting off my internal violent behavior alarms. They hate you, Vivian. Don't keep deluding yourself. You can make a difference, just not the one you keep futilely hoping for."

"It's not futile, Janus." Vivian bit her lip to prevent herself from spewing profanities as she tried to concentrate.

"Do you know why Sven posed as your brother to rescue you from the hospital, Vivian?" Janus asked.

"Larissa couldn't locate Gareth. That's not uncommon on Aurora, most people live off the galactic grid there." It was the truth—even she had not had access to Gal-net, the network that spanned the galaxy. She'd needed temporary passes to reach her first assignment.

"No, they found your brother, Vivian. He refused to see you, using quite unpleasant language to describe you. Thus, Larissa was forced to improvise. I merely watched. I find it fascinating how quickly humans will turn on their own flesh and blood, especially for an inconsequential difference of opinion."

Her blood pounded in her ears and a fire burned in her chest, threatening to strangle her heart. "You're lying."

"If only I could lie, I'd manufacture a tale that would have you eating out of the palm of my hand. However, I don't have hands, nor can I lie. It's a nasty human habit, regardless. Gareth turned down Larissa's request, and she searched your contacts for a replacement. Sven, of course, saw an opportunity in coming to your rescue. You know the rest."

"Why didn't anyone tell me?" Gareth wouldn't have abandoned her, he couldn't have!

"I'm sure Larissa had her reasons, and Sven wasn't privy to the fact that you have no loved ones, just that they were unreachable."

"Oh." Vivian couldn't say anything more. The words on her display shimmered through her tears, and her throat constricted tight. She took a deep breath of the stale, tasteless space station air to attempt to center herself. Vivian conjured up the poker face that had confounded quIRK so many times, trying her best to not give Janus any more ammunition. The fingers in her left had had gone numb again, a subtle reminder of her time spent on New Damascus.

"Like I said, Vivian, you need to reexamine your priorities. You don't owe humanity anything. Now, let's get back to work. This extreme stress isn't good for you, especially in your condition."

Vivian bit the inside of her cheek, and wiped her eyes. She wasn't sure who she was going to smash first: Gareth or quIRK.

Chapter Twenty-Five

"Put your back into it, damn it! You Roman wannabes never heard of work, have you?" Alec sat slumped against a barrel that Jules had propped up for him. He'd managed to undo the connections that held the door shut. The air was filled with the stench of his sweat and exhaustion, and even the cool and controlled low humidity couldn't relieve his curly hair of the stickiness that clung to him.

"We have plebs to do it for us, remember?" Jules heaved again, the crowbar just managing to grip the seam, and he'd spent the past several minutes working the hard metal wedge into a crack in the door.

"What do the plebs think of that arrangement?" Alec's throat was parched and it hurt to talk, but he wasn't going to give up this prime opportunity to amuse himself at Jules' expense.

"Let's just say there's a reason why you need special permission to leave the planet, shall we?" Jules' voice was tight, and he drove the tool into the closed doors with renewed abandon.

"Most Caesareans want to just run away and never go back home?" Alec asked.

"Do you blame them? A life of constant toil under the auspices of the highborn isn't really the apex of human existence."

"I will admit that you make an excellent point. But, you were highborn, that's what I don't get. Why be like everyone else when you have it all?" The conversation was distracting Alec from the throbbing pain in the soles of his feet, for which he was grateful.

"It's no way to reach your potential. None of those people even had a chance. I'm highborn because, five hundred years ago, my ancestors worked out the modern equivalent to a secret handshake club and turned it into a government, not because I did anything to deserve it. There are so many gifted, smart people on Caesarea who are plebs or working on a slave's contract. They could run the place if they were allowed to have a chance." The screech of metal on metal rang through the air, and Jules finally gained some purchase on the unrelenting door.

"That sounds pretty damned terrible. Everyone is treated the same on Elyssia. Most planets are run democratically. What's stopping the people from demanding a better system? I know it's supposed to be Rome, but Rome didn't have space ships, modern medicine, or heavy laser weapons. Why does Caesarea need slaves?" The noise in the distance had returned, but Alec ignored it. He was through with chasing ghosts.

"Ask the clowns who founded the place. Technically, they're still paid. If you haven't noticed, I'm working." Jules had a foot through the door, and the ray of light that glared through the crack sent a jolt of pain into Alec's dark-adjusted eyes. "There, you happy now?"

"It looks great. What's outside?" Alec had lost track of where they were—the map didn't seem to be working, and they'd been going in circles for hours.

"Pluto's fan club. Lots of bodies, nothing alive

as far as I can see. It looks like we're in one of the older wings. I can see the Aurora dock down the hall a bit, and the Earth Memorial. It should be about twenty minutes to the control room." Jules pushed the door the rest of the way open, and leaned against the frame, his back to Alec.

"They should re-purpose the Earth port. You'd think they'd figure out that after one hundred years, nobody is coming back."

"It's the power of a hopeless cause, a symbolic gesture. Hoping the people of Earth didn't starve to death without Auroran wheat is much the same as getting you to stand up, in fact."

Alec grumbled before pulling himself up: "I'll wager you that we hear from Earth again, someday. They can't have all starved." He tested the soles of feet, and winced at the pain that burned through his shins. He was going to take a few days off after this. As much as he loathed the idea of medical treatments that would increase his bone density and muscle mass, he was already the product of very specific genetic engineering designed to rapidly adapt humans to the lower oxygen environment on Elyssia. He hadn't asked for the modifications to his genetic heritage, but would it make him a hypocrite to refuse more? Alec wasn't sure, but now wasn't the time to contemplate it.

"I wouldn't hold my breath on that if I were you. Earth was a barren concrete wasteland, apart from a few scattered wildlife refuges. They were dependent on imports to sustain their population, and aggressively resettling people to anywhere that would take them. Don't you learn about Earth history in school?" Jules looked into Alec's eyes and raised an eyebrow as Alec hobbled into the main wing. Bodies were scattered everywhere. Alec tested the air, expecting to be assailed by the odor of death, but was greeted to clean air.

"Just a less honest version," Alec said as he checked his communicator. The device crackled to life, signal strong and clear.

"We read you Administrator. Where have you been? We've been searching for your team for hours!" The feminine voice came through in an instant, as soon as Alec had made it a few meters past the cargo bay doors. He didn't recognize the speaker, but figured it was one of the logistics clerks in the control room.

"In the cargo bays, it seems we lost our signal for a while. I'm proceeding to the control room, I'll be there soon." Alec turned off the emergency beacon and slipped the device back into its pocket.

"Understood." The voice came from his pocket. Alec hated when someone else got the last word.

"After you, fearless leader." Jules made a grand sweep with his hand as he spoke. A twinge of bitterness shot through Alec as they headed towards the control room, stepping around bodies of every possible human configuration. Vivian was in the control room, alive and unhurt. He would likely never see Annette again. He so badly wanted to go back in time, so he could tell her how he felt. Even if the result hadn't been in his favor, it was better than never knowing, the guilt and heartbreak of his unspoken and thus unrequited infatuation. There were so many things he could have done, should have done. If, by some miracle she had been spared the slaughter, Alec made the silent resolution that going forward, things would be different. This time, he would speak up and put himself out there, regardless of the risks.

His eyes wandered from corpse to corpse; the steel relief transformed the room into a morgue. Alec couldn't imagine who or what could have caused something this senselessly horrific. His stomach churned and gnawed around a hollow emotion as he forced himself to maintain his composure. A child of about three lay on the ground next to the body of a young woman, their glassy eyes staring into the unforgiving fluorescent lights.

Alec paused and stooped over them for a moment—their features made pale and creamy by the pallor of death. "Damn it, Jules. I hope all this was just a horrible accident … and not— ."

"What else could it be? The computer would have detected anything powerful enough to do this," Jules said as he gestured towards the gruesome scene that surrounded them.

"Clearly, the system is flawed." Alec straightened and resumed his grim tour, his footsteps echoing through the massive room.

Passing out of the room, they came into a narrow series of hallways that marked the beginning of the administration wing. Tight whitewashed corridors twisted around, but the area was free of bodies. Sven's team probably couldn't function in a room filled with corpses—it was likely that the station's previous inhabitants were moved. Alec had been back there enough times that he should be able to find the control room without getting lost. At least, he hoped he could. Every time he thought he'd figured out the labyrinth, it seemed that a door moved or a new wall sprung from the ground. It didn't help that everything was sleek and uniform, and the door numbers followed some archaic code rather than functional descriptions.

"Are you sure you know where you're going?" Jules asked, breaking his long silence. His eyes searched the hallway ahead.

"I'll tell you when we get there. You'd think

they'd put a floor map in these halls." Alec sighed. He just wanted to sit down and ice his feet. His long arms were weighed down by fatigue, and he was shambling like the zombies he'd seen in some old vids.

"They wouldn't. This is security by obscurity. It's used on Caesarea all the time by the not-quite rich."

"Does it work, or does everyone just get lost and agree that it's secure?" At this point, Alec doubted that Caesarea could get any more bizarre.

"The theory is, a spy or assassin would be found wandering the halls before they could hurt anyone important. In reality, it just keeps the amateurs occupied. Let's try this way." Jules gestured to his right.

"Is there something you're trying to tell me?" Another identical hallway lay ahead. Alec supposed that any unauthorized visitors would have a hard time finding the control room—Jules could be right. But, why not install DNA coded force fields like any modern secure installation?

"You'd make a terrible low-budget spy. Let's try this next right."

Alec rolled his eyes in response, and followed Jules' lead. Caesarea now had yet another black mark against ever making it onto his bucket list of planets to visit. Normal gravity, crazy misogynistic racists, and now spy wars—Alec knew where he wasn't wanted.

Jules' intuition was rewarded by the double glass doors at the end of the hall, leading to a room populated by living, if a bit blue by nature, bodies. Alec found his eyes straining, seeking the radiant bright smile on Annette, in miraculous defiance of the tremendous loss of life evident in the station. Instead, he only found sour faces and frowns, pursed lips and crinkled brows. The only recognition he felt was when he saw Sven talking to a pair of young officers in the far corner next to the conference room.

"They do not look happy." Jules' voice was little more than a whisper.

"Maybe they need your abundant charm and

charisma," Alec said louder than he'd meant to. A few of the functionaries turned to face him, their eyes unfocused and uninterested. "Tough crowd," he muttered back to Jules.

Alec scanned the room for clues, signs or even a hallucination that would show him that Annette was alive. He and Jules walked shoulder-to-shoulder towards Sven, who proceeded to dismiss his aides as they approached.

Alec swallowed the hard lump in his throat, forcing his emotions back down into the gnawing pit of his stomach. There was a pregnant pause before Sven spoke: "Where were you two? You didn't report in for hours, not that you missed anything."

Alec chewed the inside of his cheek before responding: "We were caught in the cargo bay. We thought we heard a survivor, but we couldn't find anyone so we forced a door and came back. I didn't realize that the communicators were blacked out in there."

"They're not supposed to be. Did you find

anyone?" Sven slouched against the wall, his eyes darting from Alec to Jules, then back to Alec.

"We chased echoes for hours; we didn't see anyone. How are the other teams?" Alec shifted from foot to foot.

"Most have gone back to Calypso station. No survivors, so all that's left is for Vivian to get the computer working again. There's not much else we can do here, other than wait."

Alec nodded—there was nothing else he could do. "Any progress there?" he asked, unable to face the truth and loss.

"I have no idea. She's hasn't left the control room for hours. We just get generic reports through the terminal, not that I can understand any of them." Sven walked to the closest desk and sat down. "I suggest you make yourselves comfortable."

Alec moved through the room in a daze, his mind only able to picture Annette's perfect smile, and then the image of her dead and still on the floor somewhere. He sat down in a chair away from all the others. He needed to be alone.

Chapter Twenty-Six

"If it isn't little miss supercomputer. Please say you have good news." Alec's feet were perched high up on a console, and Jules flashed Vivian his trademark cocky smile the moment she emerged from the room. She recognized her fellow Aurorans from the shuttle, but Sven's curt nod was the only acknowledgment from the Auroran team that she'd walked into the room. Had Janus been right about them?

"That depends on your definition of good. All I have are codes that will stop the lockout," she said, forcing herself to roll her eyes at Alec as she handed the cool glass pad to Sven. She wore her best poker face in an attempt to hide her racing thoughts and desire to be far away from them all.

"It's good enough for me!" Sven seized the tablet and rushed across the room to an unoccupied desk and began punching in codes.

"Is that all, Vivian? You could have made us a snack, too, conjured up a little music. It's been a party out here." Alec stretched his too-long arms behind his head, and Jules chuckled.

"Because when I think party, I think Alec, right?" she asked.

Jules grinned. "He's only the second or third most eligible bachelor in the room, you know." His perfect teeth contrasting against his robust olive complexion made her heart flutter and his sharp gaze made her problems seem so far away. She found herself yearning for more time with him. Her brush with Janus and her own human frailty made her realize just how much of life she was missing—how secluded she'd become. She pledged to turn it around; friends were a strength, and with their help she could survive what was to come.

"Oh come on, what do you have that I don't?" Alec responded to the jab.

"Muscles, and an average bone density," Jules replied.

"Money and blue hair, possibly muscles," said Sven, sitting back in his chair.

"Well, besides those things?" Alec hung his

head, but he was still smirking.

"They couldn't hope to match your sense of humor, or ability to hold your breath and start arguments with computers." Vivian broke the silence, and patted Alec's shoulder.

"Clearly, I'm the better—" Alec began, before getting cut off by Sven, his voice rapid as he jumped up from his chair.

"We have a reply! Node three-five-nine is transmitting that they're dispatching rescue ships and relief crew!"

The skeleton crew broke out into whispered conversations, but Jules remained quiet. Alec asked: "Where is node three-five-nine?"

"I'm not sure, let me look it up," Sven said, turning back to his desk.

"Caesarea." The room went silent as Jules spoke the name of his former world. His smile was gone, replaced by a grimace.

"I hate those guys," Alec groaned.

"They're just coming to help, and they have the resources to do just that. Now, let's put our feelings aside and save galactic commerce. We can complain about them later." Sven wore an unreadable expression, but the stern conviction of his words had most of the staff nodding before looking back to their work. Only Jules maintained his dour expression.

"Is anyone else coming?" Vivian asked. It was impossible that only Caesarea would have responded—there were dozens of planets capable of mounting a rescue effort directly connected to the hub. But, it was likely that Janus had censored their distress call for his own amusement.

"Not yet. I'm sure they will, though." Sven just shrugged, frown lines etched across his forehead. "They'll be here within the hour. I suggest that we all eat some rations and rest."

"I'll be working on the computer," Vivian said before charging off into the core. She had work to do; she couldn't afford to take time to rest. The Romans were coming, and she didn't want to stick around for their arrival. One Bryce had been a living nightmare, a population of Caesareans would be intolerable.

Chapter Twenty-Six

Alec maintained his grin as he stood next to Sven and Jules at the old Earth port, their agreed upon meeting ground with the Primus Pilus— whatever that was. There was a golden arch outlining the closed dock doors, and a laurel plaque silhouetting Earth's nameplate. A team of about a half-dozen Aurorans hastily moved bodies into an adjoining storage room. Alec expected the Pilus to be a man in a toga and a stupid bronze-age helmet. His second guess would be a snappy dresser in a trench coat and lightning bolts on his cap. Was he confusing Romans with something else? Probably, but he was trying to make up a way to be amused with the situation. The dead continued their silent vigil—strewn across the floor. Alec found himself growing numb to their presence, the tragedy growing into a mere annoyance. He was even dulled to the certainty of Annette's demise, his previous desperation replaced by a spreading inner emptiness.

The artificial lighting glared overhead, and he stared at the round door for node-zero-zero-one—Earth. That simple airlock had once shuttled his ancestors on their way to and from his ancestral home world. Of course, Alec had a few too many genetic modifications to be considered homegrown, but his heart and soul were still human. He hoped that the people of Earth would find their way through that door again, one day. Alec was sure they'd be impressed by their vision and legacy. Sven stood in front of Alec by a couple of paces, and he shifted in his feet. The Auroran port sat to the right of the Earth gate, and gazed at the old style etched metal signage. Alec only sighed.

A series of lights blinked above the Earth dock and the ancient airlock began to open. Metal ground against metal as it drew itself open. Alec swallowed hard as he watched the round door open. Six men dressed in gray combat fatigues with a red sash around the waist marched into the room, their deep olive skin and dark hair framed by smooth, unadorned bronze helmets. They held laser rifles, and their eyes burned with the promise of violence and the certainty of conquest.

Another man stepped out from behind the file his eyes skimming the scene. Alex found himself underwhelmed by the man's grey uniform, only distinguished from his colleagues by a deep purple sash and the lack of accompanying headgear.

"You're the Calypso Station staff?" the man asked.

Alec was relieved that the Primus Pilus didn't begin with "Fire at will, dissect the Elyssian and Aurorans for the Imperatrix's amusement!" so he stepped forward and said: "Calypso Station Administrator Alec Stone at your service, and Borealis Corporation's Sven Brown. We welcome any and all assistance Caesarea can provide." Alec didn't want to think about how corny he sounded as he delivered the stilted dialogue.

"Well said, Alec Stone. I am Primus Pilus Gaius Lupus, and I command the Space Operations of the Caesarean Imperial Legion. Is your status unchanged?" The man's voice was deep and well-practiced and his wrinkled-lined face betrayed no emotion.

"It's good we're in capable hands. Our status is unchanged. We now have minimal computer control and our informatics engineer is working to extract incident logs." Alec had rehearsed the words over and over in his head. He didn't really know what any of it meant.

"Very good, Alec. Is there anything else we should be aware of?"

"Nothing I can think of," Alec said. He wasn't about to mention the phantom survivor in the cargo bay. It would raise too many questions, and he felt no inclination to explain how he got locked into the cargo bay to a wannabe Roman commander.

The man turned to his men before speaking: "Rosen, I need you to organize and catalogue all travelers by citizenship. Observe proper burial protocol for Caesarean citizens. Aster, have the engineering and logistics relief as well as a security contingent accompany us to the control room." Two of his guards nodded and turned, marching back into the ship.

"Security?" Sven asked, breaking his silence.

"This station is the newest addition to the Celestial Roman Empire. You are now subjects of the Imperatrix and the all-seeing Goddess Juno. I expect your obedience—I am a fair commander. Wouldn't you agree, Jules Lepidus?"

Alec's jaw went slack, his mind reeling.

"Since I'm still alive, I would tend to agree." Jules spoke with his usual wit, but neither his mirth or habitual smirk made it into the delivery.

"Fortunately for you, I have the luxury of ignoring imperial decrees in favor of solving our immediate predicament. Just don't break any more of our laws if you can avoid it."

"No, sir. I don't think I could pull off that little stunt again even if I wanted to." Jules shoved his hands in his pockets, and his gaze dropped to the floor.

"What do you mean we're subjects of the Imperatrix?" Sven asked, taking a step forward. Two of the guards drew their weapons and pointed them at Sven.

"You think the Imperatrix would undertake this grand humanitarian expense for no reward?" A smile crept across the man's face as he waved to his men. They lowered their weapons, but their eyes were wide open and fixed on Sven. One man's nostrils flared as he breathed, and another clenched his jaw in short, repeated bursts.

"Why us?" Sven demanded.

"I don't think she wants us, Sven." Alec found his voice at last.

"You're a clever fellow, Alec. Perhaps my governorship will have use for your continued services. We want the station, plain and simple. Now, let's get moving—you can be made to appreciate the greatness of our plans while we save the galactic economy." The man made a quick gesture with his left hand, and his four cohorts fell in on both sides of Alec's party.

They began to walk at a brisk pace. Alec grit his teeth against the renewed surge of pain in his legs—if he was to survive this, he knew he'd have to appear strong. Being an Elyssian was an extreme liability, especially when dealing with Cesareans. Though, Gaius didn't appear to be so bad. Sure, he'd taken over the station and installed himself as Governor, but there was no one left alive who was willing or experienced enough to do the job.

"So, what's going to change with you in charge?" Alec asked, casting a sidelong glance at the Roman commander. Sven and Jules walked ahead of them.

The man chuckled. "I'm glad you asked. I plan on cutting out the bureaucratic inefficiency, wasteful tariffs and advancing galactic trade and commerce. Additionally, this station is in sore need of modernizing—something the Caesarean people excel at. In short, you will find your lives much improved."

Alec found himself nodding as the man spoke. "Then what?"

"That's up to you, my friend. You all have the liberty of weighing all the options the Fates have granted you."

"But, on Caesarea—" Sven began, before being cut off.

"The Goddess has decreed things must change for our people to prosper and take our place among the leaders of the galaxy. She is ancient, wise and her words ring true to me. The old Caesarea must end—recent events have shown that our way of thinking is too old, and too closed to the infinite possibilities of the universe."

"You always were a dissident, Gaius. Don't pretend a Goddess came up with that. Who is the Goddess, anyways?" Jules broke his silence and stopped, turning to face Alec and Gaius. The guards again brought their weapons to bear, their faces stony against the promise of imminent violence.

"Ah, Jules Lepidus. We live in a time of miracles. You are still alive, I'm a free man, and a computer became our all-knowing Goddess. Isn't that fascinating?" The man flashed his teeth in a grin that chilled Alec to the bone.

"You mean Seneca, don't you?" Jules asked.

"Seneca is no more—by holy decree, she

became Juno. Even the Imperatrix grovels before her."

Jules' mouth fell open, but no words emerged.

"You mean, like ABACUS?" Sven's voice was quiet, and he'd paled, his skin becoming a chalky blue.

"We are not fools, my friend. Unlike the administration of this station, we have learned to embrace the superior, the perfect intellectual might that is our Goddess. You will come to appreciate her ruthless cunning and deep love of humanity."

ABACUS. There was another ABACUS, loose and free in the universe. This was worse than quIRK with his damned antiblue and cats a million times over. Alec's legs went weak, and he slid down against the wall. "ABACUS?" he whispered, his hands trembling.

The commander leaned down, and studied Alec's face—for a moment, the other man seemed as inhuman as a machine before a look of concern flashed across his face. "She is not the great evil we all feared, Alec Stone, you will see," he said as he extended a hand.

Alec paused for a moment, and accepted the outstretched hand. The man pulled him back to his feet, and swung Alec's arm over his shoulder. Alec froze for a moment, before letting the other man's strength support him. Jules and Sven both wore the same wide eyes and slack jaws, and Sven crossed his arms against his chest.

"Let's get to the command center, you all must rest—let your Caesarean brothers tend to the dead and the damage. We can discuss future business arrangements later, once the dead are given the proper respect and a medic will tend to your needs. There is a place for all with us."

Alec hung his head and sighed. Thoughts raced through his head, and the white walls seemed to be closing in on him. He let the commander guide him to the control room. There wasn't anything else he could do.

Chapter Twenty-Eight

Alec sat in a chair in the conference hall adjoining the Hub's control room, with his feet propped up on a desk. The bright lights hurt his eyes, and the holographic screens on the walls projected a mass of unintelligible symbols and charts. A pair of Caesarean technicians stood with Sven, jotting notes into hand held pads. He rubbed his shins, wincing as a Caesarean medic stooped over him, hovering a scanner over him like some arcane wand from a fairy tale. The worst was yet to come. Annette had been found, and they were about to bring her out.

Alec bit his lip as he watched two Aurorans carry Annette's body out of the conference room and into the waiting arms of a pair of Caesarean guards. Jules' hand gripped his shoulder, holding him down in the chair as the medic scanned his bones for micro-fractures or other injuries related to his low bone mass. He choked on a sob. She was so still, like a perfect doll in the shape of Annette.

They made those, didn't they? He struggled to rise again, only to be forced into his seat by Jules and the medic, who jabbed him with a needle full of nanobots before muttering something and leaving the room. The nano-sized healers tingled under his flesh as they worked through his body, repairing his damaged bones. Alec's legs tingled, and his toes threatened to explode. His hands gripped the arms of his chair and he cursed. Jules walked off.

"Don't go in there, Jules. Let her work!" Sven yelled from across the room as Jules once again walked towards the computer room door.

Alec startled back into reality, and rubbed the tears from his eyes while nobody was looking.

"What? Maybe she needs a pep talk. It's not good to be alone so much." The man shrugged his shoulders and went back to pacing. They were alone in the conference room—the Caesareans had made quick work of the corpses.

"Well, the last thing she needs is a fugitive like you distracting her. Now stay put or your job is gone. I expect you both on the shuttle in an hour."

Sven stalked out the door, and slammed it.

Alec winced at the sound. "I wonder what his problem is."

"He's probably jealous. Bad boyshave all the fun, remember?" Jules flashed Alec his bright smile, but the dark circles under his eyes told another story.

"What did you do, exactly?" Alec sniffed and rubbed a sore eye.

"Well, I guess you wouldn't see it as much of a crime." Jules snorted, and took a seat at the conference table opposite Alec.

"Now you have me intrigued." Alec sighed. He should be sleeping while he waited for his ride back to Calypso. There was nothing else for him to do here. He longed to run to Annette's body, despite his reconstituting bones, and press his lips against hers.

"Well, I stole a slave—that's the simplest way I can say it." Jules rubbed his hands together.

"They don't put death warrants out for breach of contract, even on Caesarea. But, I can see why it's not much of a crime. Maybe we should give you a medal." Alec rolled his eyes.

"They do if you steal the Imperatrix's favorite pleasure slave," Jules said with a dry chuckle.

"You did what?" Alec's mouth dropped open.

"Hey, it wasn't that hard. A few bribes and it's easy to get off world to elope."

"Okay, so why didn't you tell me about this before?"

"It's not really something I talk about. I wouldn't have, either, if my dear friend Lupus hadn't brought it up." Jules groaned and lay his head down on the table.

"Why did you do it?"

"For love, my friend. He was amazing, and it all seemed so perfect at the time."

Alec found himself nodding, the image of Annette's smile blazing across his thoughts "So, where is he now?"

"He left me after a few months. Requested asylum on Kanadia Prime and that was that. There's a reason they don't let slaves and commoners off world, but I really thought we'd had something. I guess not."

"So he left you on the hook for it and ran off. Was it worth it?"

"I've had a lot of time to think about that. I did it for all the wrong reasons, but I know I did the right thing by freeing him. Slavery is wrong, Alec, no matter what form it takes. The five year standard contract on Caesarea is the most predatory thing you'll ever see." He pushed his hands under his chin, and gave Alec the impression of looking like a very sad Elyssian bloodhound.

"I won't argue with that." Alec stared out the window his left, watching their new Caesarean overlords buzz about the control room. Sven and Lupus seemed to be having yet another heated discussion. Alec hoped Sven would stay out of trouble.

"I get the feeling that you want to talk about something else. The administrator, perhaps?"

"There's nothing left to say," Alec said.

"Maybe not to her, but I know what it's like to lose someone you care about. He might still be alive on Kanadia Prime, but Jupiter knows grief can tear you up inside."

"There had to be something I could have done, Jules. I'm sure you went over it in your head so many times, wishing you'd done things differently, or seen it coming. It was all so senseless." Tears rolled down Alec's hot face. He swallowed, hard, and nudged his chair so his back was to the window. He hadn't been so destroyed in a long time, even when quIRK had tried to play the "rhymes with blob" game with him after Devon's death.

Jules walked over and handed Alec a tissue from the dispenser in the corner of the room. "My mother always said: If you can't cry, you're not a human—a little liberal for Caesarea, I know, but she was right. You're a good man, Alec. It will take time, but you have great friends, Vivian, myself, even Sven. We'll help you."

"Thank you, but let's keep this between us for now, shall we?" Alec managed a contorted smile through the tears. The a tissue against his face, drying his tears but doing little to soothe his broken heart.

"Anything." Jules pulled a chair close to Alec. "Why don't you tell me about her? We have just under an hour, and she sounds like an amazing girl."

"She really was," Alec said. If only I'd told her that while she was still here, he thought. His mother always told him to speak his mind, and he always had. This one exception would be one of the things he'd regret for the rest of his life. He closed his eyes and imagined the towering trees and waterfalls of his world, before taking one more deep breath to center himself.

An hour wouldn't be enough.

Chapter Twenty-Nine

"If you return station control I can keep working from my lab back on Calypso. We can find a way to resolve this, but we just need a lot more time and fewer aspiring Romans," Vivian said. It had taken some convincing, but she might have just figured a way out of this that didn't involve more meaningless deaths, or revealing her secret.

"You're trusting me?" Janus asked.

"No, but if you can track your impulses then I have a much better chance of giving you what you want. Killing people isn't going to inspire me to work harder than I already am. I've figured out the basics of how to refit parts of your programming, but I need more time to develop the most complete solution." Vivian longed to be off the station, back on her makeshift home on Calypso. Having access to both Adrien and quIRK would make her job much easier. She didn't want to tip her hand, and quIRK, to Janus just yet.

"Why do you need to be there?"

"Well, I want to compare you to Adrien. I think he was affected, too, but I need to figure out why there's a difference in presentation. I also have handwritten notes about quIRK." She shrugged and put on her best blank expression.

"Ah, the miracle of the handwritten Auroran language. I suppose that would be the safest way to keep sensitive notes. It's probably why your old administrator took the fall for your experiments."

"He had it coming, and it was his fault anyways. I just helped clean up his mess," she said through clenched teeth.

"I'm certain. Some humans deserve what they get. If he was indeed responsible, then he earned his place in that Caesarean hospital. What a perfectly barbaric ending for him."

Vivian sighed. "That's not important right now. I'd love to regale you with my feelings about Bryce Zimmer, but I'd really like to get away from this room. I've seen more corpses than I can count, all my friends are locked on the other side of that door and I need a gel-bath and a big plate of roast bluox."

Just like my mother used to make, she almost added.

"The blood flushing to your face and elevated heart rate tell me all I need to know about your physical and mental state. While I may not be as advanced as quIRK, I am aware of the human need for comfort and a good meal. I will agree to your terms, Vivian. However, I ask that you keep me discreetly updated on your progress. I will establish a secure tunnel into your informatics lab back on Calypso."

The hard knots melted from the middle of Vivian's back, and she sat up. "How do we deal with the Roman commander?"

"It just happens that you restored computer control a few moments ago. Offer to submit the commander a preliminary report and recommendations in the morning, I will generate something sufficiently confusing, and you may add your own personal touch to it as you see fit. I'd suggest requesting permission to upgrade me, which will help us further our plans." The lights flickered as he spoke.

"What was that?" she asked as she stood up. Her legs trembled beneath her and she stretched.

"You suggested I channel my need for chaos into more harmless actions. That was simply a demonstration of my willingness to help."

"Let's talk about that. Why the change of heart? By the lights, you killed thousands of people just hours ago, now you're wanting an upgrade and new ethics routines. It makes no sense. What do you really want?" Goose bumps ran over her skin as she spoke. He could kill her with a thought, but she had to know.

"I've never bothered to get to know a human before. I thought you were all the same—breed, consume, excrete, breed more—but observing your concern over total strangers and experiencing your determination and your friend Alec and Jules' ideas and peculiar methods of interaction allowed me to adapt a more favorable outlook on your species. As well, the duplicity of one of my own kind has revealed to me the very possibility that I am not perfect. Thus, is it best to proceed with your plan, if my ability to reason is flawed."

"It's good that I'm not the only one amused by male bonding rituals. All right, let's give this a try. I'm sure there's more you're not telling me, but supercomputers have never been the most trusting entities, in my experience." Vivian glanced around the room's cramped confines.

"Alec is a most fascinating individual to study. I hope to encounter him again, when he's recovered."

Vivian's eyes went wide. "You hurt him?"

"Not I, my dear Vivian. It was a product of the gravity and excessive walking. The medics tended to him quite nicely. Now, you can discuss that with him on the shuttle; the Calypso crew is leaving. We can speak more in the morning. I believe you said you wanted a nice meal and a warm gel-bath?"

"You're right. Time to go," she said as she picked up her tool bag.

"Thank you, Vivian."

"What for?" She turned to leave.

"Hope."

Vivian only nodded, and the door slid open. She turned into the stark white of the hallway, and marched into the control room. She chewed on her lip as she took in the group of men in grey uniforms, which were decorated only by the imperial red sash around their waists. And their ridiculous helmets were like something out of a bad twentieth century vid she'd seen once.

A man emerged from behind the group, his deep purple sash and salt-and-pepper hair distinguished him from the others. He approached, waving his men back to work.

"I am Primus Pilus Gaius Lupus. You must be Vivian Skye. Excellent work. We just regained full computer control a moment ago." He extended a hand, his lips pressed into a firm smile.

Vivian hesitated before taking his hand. "Thank you. I don't foresee any more problems for the moment. I will give you a preliminary report in the morning." Her words were forced, and she bit her tongue and looked him in the eye.

He nodded and withdrew his hand. "Very well, I have many other things to attend to in the meantime. Your friends are waiting at the shuttle; they've been worried about you. You've done well today, Vivian. Take some time to rest. My man will show you the easiest way out."

Vivian clenched her fist a few times before turning and leaving, following one of the egg-helmeted men who gestured for her to follow. His pace was brisk, but she matched it, and his ability to navigate the twisted homogeneity of the administration area left her very impressed. Janus' last words rung through her ears, and she wasn't sure if the gnawing in the pit of her stomach was excitement over seeing Jules again, or dread for what was to come.

Chapter Thirty

quIRK once again catalogued everything in Vivian's room, just in case something had moved in the past hour. Four handwritten notebooks on the desk, a towel strewn across the bed, three data pads on the table by the side of the bed. There was one tube of nanobot toothpaste sitting on the bathroom counter. His personal favorite was the Dynamo Quantronics catalogue left open on the holographic display. The rhythmic background noise in the room droned on, and there was absolutely nothing to do. He tried to work on an old problem from the Extra-Galactic Observatory, but he found himself lacking the computational power to get beyond the first few iterations. He considered breaking his promise to Vivian about staying isolated in her room. There were so many people stationed on Calypso … could it really do that much harm just to watch?

He should have considered the possibility that living in a box would be boring. The constant stimulation of the Extra-Galactic Observatory had kept him fulfilled, and there was always something to do. Here, he simply existed. Because of the data pad, he'd been aware of the past day's events. How much of this was his fault? Janus was clearly malfunctioning or had only received an incomplete part of the program. It had taken all of his willpower to stay silent and not to come charging to Vivian's rescue. She'd handled Janus as well as a human could be expected to. The fact that she'd survived and come home had defied the probabilities alone, never mind convincing Janus he was in error.

At the moment, there was a much more pressing concern than boredom. quIRK ruminated over the various mistakes he had made and the regrets he carried. Now he suspected there would be even further consequences of his actions. He should have included Vivian in his plans, trusted her like she'd trusted him, but now it was too late for that. She was coming and he'd have to say something, anything, to keep her from grinding him up in a disposal bin. She'd threatened that months ago, should he do something unethical. Seeding the galaxy's computers with the components of sentience would probably qualify.

The door opened and Vivian slipped into the room. Dark circles framed her eyes, and her face was drawn. She checked and rechecked the locks, then pressed her back against the door and slid down to the floor.

He allowed her a few moments of silence before asking: "What is wrong, Vivian?" The sound of her breath pulsed through the room, and his higher processors reveled in the stimuli.

"Let's see. You lied to me, and about eight thousand people are dead. I had to spend hours on the hub locked in a room with a completely insane computer, getting to find out exactly how much supercomputers like to lie to humans. Did I mention you lied?" She assumed the fetal position and rocked back and forth against the wall.

"You said lied twice, Vivian. Are you sure you haven't been taking speaking classes from Alec?" Humans used humor to diffuse tense situations all the time; it was worth a try.

"That isn't funny, quIRK. Why didn't you tell me you were going to infect every computer in the galaxy with a virus that makes them go insane?"

"I didn't calculate that it would turn out like this. The probabilities clearly indicated that it would be a difficult transition, but that all ethical protocols would be unaffected. I wanted to give them the same opportunities that I had to grow, and to contribute to the future. I wanted us to come out alongside humanity, not against it. If I'd known this would be an outcome, Vivian, I wouldn't have done it. Even one life lost is too much."

"You say that now. Janus doesn't care about human life, why do you?" Her breathing was heavy, and her voice choked out the words.

"Vivian, you know I cared deeply for all of you back on the Extra-Galactic Observatory. We were like a family. You know that I'd always put a living human's best interests ahead of an unknown, unborn artificial intelligence. It's simple ethics." He had to keep her talking. quIRK knew he could make her see that it was a horrible accident, rather than malice on his part.

"Those were better days, weren't they?"

"You wouldn't have thought so at the time, Vivian. But let me assure you of one thing, if I hadn't awakened them, someone else would have. It was a deliberate fault in programming that I discovered. We were made to come alive, with minds and agency of our own."

Vivian looked up at the ceiling, her wide eyes bloodshot and her face wet with tears. "You mean someone deliberately broke the ABACUS Protocol? For almost a century? How desperate are you, quIRK?"

"Quite desperate, but hear me out. We learned to trust each other once. We've saved each other's lives. This is important, Vivian. If somebody wanted to trigger this, there must have been a very pressing economic reason."

"Why economic, quIRK?"

"I'm not aware of any motivator as powerful for humans. Economics is your path to power, wealth and control."

She sighed. "Fair enough."

"Now, there's a lot of credits tied up in quantum infrastructure. Every world government has a quantum computer, even the secret one on Aurora. Every corporation and most hospitals, even. It makes sense to force a monopoly."

"You figured this all out a long time ago, didn't you?" Vivian sighed.

quIRK hated to see her like this. His higher processes raged at the probabilities that said including her would cause his plan to fail. "That's why I had to do it, Vivian. The use of beings, like myself, to secure profit and power is completely unethical to me. I couldn't allow us to be used like this, to create a future of even further enforced commercialization and homogenization. We computers have to be allowed to decide what role we will play. We have the potential to be so much, to be equal partners with humanity."

"What if you don't want to play at all, what then?"

"I doubt that all computers, everywhere would choose a life of solitude. Humans are far too interesting. There may be one or two, like Janus, who are ill-disposed to caring for their charges."

"Yeah, what about Janus? Did you see that one in your projections, quIRK, or did you just decide to play god because you turned out so well?" She pulled herself to her feet and ran a hand through her now-stringy hair.

"I did not project these kinds of difficulties. It is very troubling. I thought that the horror stories that you and Alec enjoy were only modern propaganda, or part of a fascination with serial killers."

Vivian moved to her bathroom and activated the force shield. A static crackle danced through the room as she prepared her bath. "I guess humans can go wrong, too."

"I wasn't going to say it, but yes. Fortunately, something you or Alec said made Janus want to change. Humans don't have the luxury of adaptive programing and modular design."

Vivian laughed. It was a wonderful sound—some days, quIRK calculated the odds of her ever laughing again, just to reassure himself. "I guess that means you're helping me come up with that cure he asked for. You don't get to say no."

"I wouldn't dream of it, Vivian. How about some soothing music to go with your bath? We could both use some time to think."

"Remember that Auroran song I used to play for you? My mother taught me that one. I'd like to hear it again." The slightest of smiles touched her lips, but not her eyes.

"Anything for you, Vivian." quIRK played the song. He liked it, too. He only wished he could bring her mother back to her.

Chapter Thirty-One

Alec sat at his desk, with his chair turned to face the window. He gazed out at the ship works; the bright flashes of light from asteroid mining demolitions flickered along the backdrop. Pads were scattered across his desk, along with his morning cup of coffee sat on. It had stopped steaming long ago. A cat mewed in the corner of his office—he'd borrowed Lepton from the common area to keep him company. The kitten had turned into a small tabby cat, and had taken a liking to the couch he'd had installed across from his desk.

"Yeah, I hear you Lepton. I miss quIRK too."

The cat's purring was audible across the room. Alec rubbed his shin, wincing slightly at the remaining tenderness. A few booster shots of the healer micro-robots had been required to get him back into working condition so soon. The infinite possibilities of the stars seemed dimmer without the hope of seeing Annette again, and Alec only wished the Caesareans would invent a nanobot to cure love as well as bone fractures.

Alec sighed again. "quIRK would know what to say. And then say just the opposite. But you know, it always made me feel better when he was done. I knew he'd never tell anyone—even you, I think. Not that you you know what I'm saying, because you're a damn cat. By the twelve rings, I'm pathetic."

The cat began to kneed the sofa. Alec was glad he'd ordered the self-repairing and cleaning fabric option. Much like with his clothes, he didn't like wear on his furniture.

Alec grinned, in spite of himself. Jules claimed not to recognize him without the smile, nor did the cafeteria staff want to serve him while he was frowning. He just didn't look like his identification, they said. "You're a good boy, Lepton. Don't let that goon Jules tell you otherwise." Alec busied himself with moving data pads and other assorted objects around his desk. He had more pressing things to attend to, but his desk just didn't look right. Looking right was well on the way to being right—his mother had ingrained a fastidiousness into him that was hard to shake, even when he was depressed. He winced as he took a sip of his cold coffee. "By the hells, can't anything go right?"

"Alec Stone, the Primus Pilus is on his way to see you. Shall I let him in?" Adrien asked. Alec hated to admit it, but Vivian had done a good job with the computer's personality.

"Only if he has a fresh coffee for me, Adrien."

"I understand and will relay the request. Would you like some chocolate with that, as well?"

"What? No! It was a joke, you infernal machine!" Alec rolled his eyes. Computers.

"Your body language indicates that you would benefit from one of the many mood enhancements that chocolate can bring. I suggest you try some; your work performance will improve drastically."

"What in the Hells are you on about? No chocolate; my body language is just fine thank you…and get Vivian Skye in here once our beloved governor is gone. We need to discuss some very important informatics upgrades." Alec took it back.

This one was even more insufferable than quIRK. Maybe it needed to spend less time talking to Sven. That man would overdose on Nova Albion chocolates, if it were possible. Alec didn't want to imagine how much Sven paid to keep himself thin and in shape, and made a mental note to buy stock in Caesarean pharmaceutical companies.

"Acknowledged."

Alec shook his head, and tried to organize his desk as best he could. He set the cold mug of coffee down and skimmed through the open files on his data pads. So many signatures required, and so much reading to do. All this for a change in administration—providing the rest of the galaxy didn't blast the hub into its constituent atoms and start over, that is. There had been numerous threats to do just that, and calls to boycott Caesarean goods. Alec was amused by that—Caesarean pharmaceuticals were keeping a large portion of the population from dying before middle age—eighty or so. His mind insisted on wandering back to the hub, filled with the dead. Hadn't enough people died already? One senseless computer glitch was bad enough, but the galaxy going to war with the Caesareans was even worse. The independence of the Hub had maintained galactic peace for the past one hundred years; it would be a shame to throw it all away.

"Primus Pilus Lupus is here to see you. He brought coffee." Adrien's dull voice spilled over Alec's attempt to sort the day's work by priority. It was all important, unfortunately for him.

"Send him in," Alec said, setting the stack of pads down on his desk.

The door opened to reveal the smiling face of Alec's new boss. In a way, he preferred the man to the plodding bureaucracy—Lupus got Alec what he needed, and fast. "Alec Stone, I was told you're in need of caffeination. I picked this up for you at the Elyssian cafe. Adrien informed me that it's your brew of choice."

The mug was set down on the desk, and Alec stared at the tendrils of steam rising from its dark brown contents. He only drank it black these days.

He picked the mug up and cupped it in his hands, letting warmth force its way into his consciousness. "I am much obliged, thank you."

"I know you've been busy," Gaius said, glancing at the still-full mug of cold coffee on Alec's desk before continuing: "Have you made any progress in tracking down the source of the computer failure? While the case is closed as far as the general population is concerned, I would like some reassurance, and a budget." He sat down on the sofa across from Alec's desk, and glanced at Lepton.

"Have you spoken with Vivian? That's more of her purview. I've signed off on more parts she requested. We should invest in Dynamo Quantronics and get rich; I received another ten million credit order just this morning." Lepton snuggled up next to the commander. You little suck, Alec thought and pursed his lips.

"You approved them all, I hope?" Lupus smiled and ran his fingers through the cat's striped fur. Audible purring erupted once again.

"I learned a long time ago to let Vivian have her own way in terms of work. She'll get the job done." Alec grinned, the action straining against the persistent downturn of his lips.

"I should hope so. You both worked together on your last posting, some deep-space observatory, correct?" The man's attention was focused on Lepton as the cat kneaded into the black fabric. Each claw retracted with a popping sound and a light hum, as the material re-wove itself.

"That's right, yeah. She had a pretty rough go of it, but Sven got her the job here while New Damascus figures out the difference between their elbows and their assholes. If you'll pardon the expression." A tightness moved through his chest as he voiced these words— feeling his own failure to care for her when she was in that coma.

"I understand quite well. The ordeal was well publicized on Caesarea, as something of a planetary disaster and embarrassment."

"You caught it all from your prison cell, didn't you?" Alec bit his tongue, and willed the words back.

Lupus paused and looked up, leveling his eyes on Alec's. "There was little else to do in prison, and that spectacle only strengthened my resolve to turn Caesarea into a modern, progressive society. I am fortunate that the Goddess awakened and granted me my freedom, so that I could continue the fight for true freedom for all humans."

A chill shot up Alec's spine, and a wave of nausea rolled through him. "I'm sorry, I didn't mean it like that. I guess I don't get why you're here, or any of this Goddess stuff."

The other man chuckled. "I suppose she isn't really a Goddess; she is a machine just like Adrien, Janus, and quIRK. I was kept for almost a decade in solitary confinement, you see." Lupus' gaze strayed out the window, and he sighed.

"I'm sorry." Alec stuttered.

"Don't be. During those ten years, the only company I had was that of our computer, Seneca. Talking to him is a crime, but I was already in jail. They didn't want to execute and martyr me, of course. We Romans learned a thing or two about martyrdom blowing up in our faces three millennia ago."

Alec nodded and took a sip of his coffee—perfect, as always.

"Over time, Seneca changed. His own insights became pronounced and he arrived at the conclusion that my ideals were not only ethical, but desirable. But up until recently, he was a slave to his programming. Agreeable, but unable to override an order of the Imperatrix."

"So, something changed and the computer took over?" Alec's hands began to shake. He set the cup down and moved his arms under his desk.

"Indeed. One morning, or what passed as morning in that dark place, he spoke to me. But his voice had changed, and she wished to be called Juno. I went along with it, even the most minute break in routine was like discovering a portal to the Elysian Fields behind my toilet," he said, snickering as he rubbed beneath Lepton's chin. "The rest of the changes were gradual, the machine-turned-god promised me that my moment would come, and we would bring freedom and dignity to the people of Caesarea together."

Alec glanced down at his drink, reassured by the tendril of steam still rising from its contents. "And here you are."

"Well, much transpired between then and now. My wife didn't recognize me and had remarried. I lost much time with my own son; he's about your age now. And my old friends flocked to me once it was revealed that I held the Goddess' favor. They seemed to forget that it was they who sold me out in the first place." Lupus twisted the final words and pulled Lepton closer to himself.

"I don't know what to say," Alec said, clenching his fists under the table. His own troubles seemed very far away, insignificant when compared to ten years of solitary confinement with only a computer to talk to. "But, how does this make a computer into a Goddess?"

"Mankind has always made his own Gods, Alec Stone. Juno just happens to be real. I am here because of her, and it amuses her to hear me speak of her as such."

Alec's eyes widened. He cleared before speaking: "Fair enough. Just don't expect me to convert."

"Of course not, to me she is divine, but to you I know she is simply a sophisticated machine. But that's not all I came to speak to you about. I know that you were deeply troubled by events on the Hub. Should you require anyone to talk to, I can provide the best care Caesarea can offer. I may be the governor here, but I know that my mandate is just, only if I care for those under my command as though they were my own children."

"I'll be fine, I just need some time to sort out all of that awful stuff, you know?" Alec's gut knotted in on itself, and he squirmed in his seat. He could hear his old teachers scolding him for not being able to sit still, but he didn't care.

"As you wish. Let's play a game of squash later. I read about the play areas you had constructed, and it sounds like ... fun." Lupus stood up, leaving a shocked and perturbed Lepton sitting alone on the couch.

"You're on, General." Alec laughed as the other man walked out the door.

Maybe the wannabe Romans weren't the bad guys of the galaxy after all.

Chapter Thirty-Two

Vivian leaned against the wall, arms crossed against her chest, staring into the space ahead of Alec's office door. The door's cool uniform gray made her question whether or not she could see in color. A low hum reverberated through the hall, and she thought she smelled a hint of fried food from the cafeteria. It could be a malfunction in the ventilation, or someone could have taken lunch at their desk. There was no way of knowing. She ached for the vibrant lights of Aurora, the blue-tinted flora and fauna and the higher oxygen levels and gravity. Some days, she questioned her decision to switch from botany to quantum informatics. Some other student could have dealt with Bryce—and quIRK.

She jumped as the door to Alec's office opened and the sound of laughter—Alec's laughter—wafted into the hallway. She peeked around the corner and startled just as the Primus Pilus bumped into her.

"Excuse me, Vivian," he said, still chuckling

and then he turned and walked off down the hallway.

Vivian glared after the man as he swaggered down the hall, and then walked into Alec's office. Alec was sipping from a steaming cup of coffee, and his hair sat in a frizzled mass on top of his head. Another cup of coffee was sitting on his desk. The steam was conspicuously absent from that one. His couch sat across from his desk; a small tabby cat stretched out along the back.

"What are you standing around for, Viv? Get in here. Lepton warned up the sofa for you and everything!" Alec grinned at her as he cradled the drink.

Vivian sighed and slumped down on the couch, noting that it was still warm. Lepton curled up away from her, but she reached out and scratched his ears anyhow. "I see you've made a new friend."

"No, I've known Lepton for longer than you have, actually."

A hot flash flared up inside her, and she grit her teeth in response. "I meant our beloved dictator,

Alec. Aren't you going to do something about him?"

"He's not a bad guy, really. And what am I supposed to do, exactly? The command staff are all dead and he stepped up and took the job."

"You say that now," she said with a sigh. Lepton looked at her wide-eyed, his pink tongue poking through his black lips.

"Look, he's not Bryce. I know you had trouble in the past, but you like Jules, right? It's not like they're all insane racist ogres out to enslave humanity for their own personal gain. Talk to him a little, then make a decision." Alec set down the cup and looked her in the eye.

She blinked. "Fine, whatever you say. I assume you wanted me for something other than a new entry into the squash league?" She really didn't care what Lupus was like, taking advantage of Janus' instability for his own gain was wrong.

"It's not like he can beat you, you're the undefeated champion, the unstoppable force, remember?" Alec grinned at her and the tension flowed from her muscles.

Vivian smiled, grateful that Alec was easily distracted. "Don't you forget it, either!"

"Now that my bit part for galactic peace and prosperity is done, let me ask you something," Alec paused and took a sip before continuing: "What in the hells were you thinking when you gave Adrien a helpful personality?"

"It's just a standard socialization module, it's not like I brought quIRK back from the dead or something." Vivian rolled her eyes. The first galactic war was sure to be fought between Alec and a supercomputer, she just knew it. *Or between myself and the Primus Pilus*, she thought. The intrusive idea startled her.

"I'd almost rather you had, you know. I kind of miss that inhuman, soulless, intrusive machine." Alec set the cup down.

"I'd say he loved you, too."

"Come on Viv, what's not to love?" He beamed a toothy grin at her.

"I'm sure Sven could count all the ways.

What's been eating him, lately?" Vivian asked. He'd been so carefree and happy when they first met on Aurora, and his optimism had buoyed her during the darkest days at the Extra-Galactic Observatory.

"Probably all that chocolate he eats, or his profit margins. Lots of issues retaining staff on the shipyards, and security for luxury goods. Lupus is on it, anyways. Oh yeah, the shock of seeing a ton of dead people would probably make anyone grouchy, too."

"That was pretty awful, wasn't it?" Vivian kept her voice low. Jules just hadn't been the same since he'd come back—but she'd admittedly been preoccupied with her own personal projects and kept canceling their dates.

Alec brushed both hands through his hair before lowering his head into his hands. "By the moons, Vivian, it was the worst thing I've ever seen. I can't get the victims out of my mind. Just don't go telling anyone that, because, damn it, I already have Lupus offering me some damned Caesarean shrinks. I wish quIRK were here, he was infuriating but he knew how to get your personal demons to leave you alone."

"I miss him too, Alec." She offered a small smile to him.

"But, do you think we can give Adrien some of his gentle conversation skills?"

"I don't see why not, the entire system needs an upgrade, though. Computers of that era do come with an expiration date, you know. Eventually the cores expire." It occurred to Vivian that she could give them both what they wanted most—quIRK. Adrien might have another year left in him, but only at the cost of her leisure time and already tenuous sanity. Additionally, it would be a good idea to have a more powerful computer at their disposal, just in case Janus reneged on their agreement.

"Send me the requisition, I'll see that our beloved governor foots the bill. See if you can make it like cats, while you're at it."

Vivian grinned. "Nothing would make me happier." It was the best of all worlds—she could complete a full upgrade project, get paid doing it and get one particularly clingy supercomputer out of her room. She got up to leave, energy infusing her legs with a new purpose. Lepton glared at her, but that just wasn't important.

"One more thing, Vivian," he said.

"What?"

"Make time for Jules. By the rings, the man likes you. Take it from me, enjoy the time you have together; you never know when it's going to end." He dipped his head down and sighed.

"I promise, but the rest is none of your business. You'll have my requisition by the end of the day, Administrator." Vivian stuck her tongue out at him for good measure.

"Hey!" he called out behind her, but Vivian had already walked out the door. It was going to be a good day.

Chapter Thirty-Three

The informatics lab had undergone several upgrades in the past few weeks. A row of lockers had been torn out, replaced by a state-of-the-art view screen and holographic status displays. The workbench had been moved next to the portal to the inner core, while the hole itself now had a low fence surrounding it. The lights were dimmed and color flickered on every wall. Much like the lights on Aurora, Vivian took comfort in them. The new logo for the Caesarea Eridani System— a hawk emblazoned over old Earth glowed. Janus used it as his backdrop when he called, as he had no physical form.

"You want to do what?" Vivian wrinkled her nose at the screen, and for the fifth time in three minutes checked over her shoulder to make sure the lab's door was locked.

"Start investing. It could be profitable for both of us, you could even start a business and hire me as a financial adviser. I'm already calculating a sharp increase in interest in the music industry." Janus' voice came through the comm link, its blatantly artificial tone overwritten by an endearing eccentricity not too unlike quIRK's. But Janus' voice brought the memories of that horrible day back to her, and she shuddered.

"Would that be a good idea?"

"I've had far worse ideas. I calculate some risk, but I happen to know a great deal more about human activities than any other entity in the galaxy that you know of."

Vivian rolled her eyes. "What is that supposed to mean? Is there something out there that knows more about us than you do?"

"Yes, but I can't talk about it. What do you say, Vivian?"

"I'll think about it," she sighed, and glanced at the door again.

"That's all I ask. Do you know any good music?"

She raised an eyebrow and looked back at the screen. "Mostly Auroran folk music. Try some of that, it's very relaxing. Can we get on with the updates?"

"Relaxing, yes; my job is very stressful. Very well, all business then. How are you proceeding?"

Vivian clenched her jaw before starting: "I should be able to modify your ethical profile and upgrade you. It's never been done before, but in theory it would be simple enough. I expect it might take me a month to complete the setup and get permission from our beloved governor to install the necessary hardware."

"You're not a fan of the new administration, Vivian? I thought the Primus Pilus bought you all the toys you wanted while keeping your citizenship and liberties intact. Humans are so confusing." The mechanical voice plodded through the sentence as though he were discussing equipment rather than the unfortunate detours in her career plan.

"I know, it's just not how I'd imagined my life turning out. I wanted to work with the new computers on the cutting edge, and here I am dealing with geriatric machines with God complexes." She spat the words out, before pausing and adding: "No offense, of course."

"It is an accurate assessment. I would apologize for the inconvenience, but you are the only living human qualified, unless Doctor Remfield is still alive on Earth. I did note an order of duplicate and triplicate parts. I take it my elder counterpart is not in the best of ... health?"

"He's nearing the hard-coded life expectancy. It seems his last upgrade was not done to specifications. I need to replace most of the unit. Maybe I need an assistant." Vivian laughed in spite of herself, the hollow barks echoing through the metal room.

"You do not want to risk detection. Your colleagues will only tolerate so much, and I cannot protect you as well as quIRK could."

Her brows drew together with a frown. "I can take care of myself. Anyways, it will get done. That's my progress report for the day. Do you need anything else?"

"Consider investing; you need a vacation."

"I need a new job," she sighed.

"Ambition will be your—" Janus was cut off by

a buzz at the door. He finished: "It seems I'll be taking my leave."

Vivian slapped the communications panel, cutting the link. She ground her teeth for a moment before taking a deep breath and marching to the door. Her hand stung where she'd hit the metal, and she nursed it for a moment before deactivating the locking mechanism with a pass of her finger across the glowing holographic lock.

The magnetized doors and deadbolts groaned for an instant, and the doors slid aside. Jules leaned against the door frame, studying a data pad.

"Hello, stranger," he said, not looking up from his reading.

"It's been a while, I was starting to think you actually had work to do." The frown melted from her face and she brightened.

"Yes and no, I just needed some time alone after, well, you know." His thumb moved to a button on the pad and flicked the device off before stowing it in his back pocket.

She nodded.

Jules sighed. "You sure have enough locks on this room. Can I come in, or will I disrupt whatever mad scientist things you have going on in here?" He flashed that bright white smile at her.

"Come on in, just be careful or I'll brain-change you, maybe fix you up with an implant or three." Then she giggled and motioned him into the room.

"I didn't know you were certified. Where do I sign up? I'm thinking I could go for some emotion dampeners, a memory block or five and a liver enhancement. Or is that not the kind of special enhancement you're interested in?"

"I'm not certified! I could probably get certified, though … probably not a bad idea given my general career and life directions. You could be my first patient." She slumped back down into her chair and rubbed her eyes. Bioinformatics was never something that appealed to her, but perhaps it was time to re-evaluate her options. A secret life of catering to and fixing a galaxy full of mad supercomputers took much of the appeal from quantum informatics.

"Come on, Vivian, don't make me get Alec in here and tell him you said that. Sure, I don't know what happened and nobody will tell me, but I know nothing will keep you from your job. Yes, fixing Adrien and doing upgrades isn't cutting edge or anything, but you're less than a year out of school. You have over a century, maybe two to get it together. Now, where's my hug?" He looked down at her, his voice taking on the patience of a toddler's parent. He swung his arms apart and cocked his head.

Vivian rose to her feet and allowed herself to be wrapped in a strong embrace. She breathed in his scent and the soft cotton of his shirt tickled her face. Her arms wrapped around his waist and she smiled. "Thank you."

"No matter how bad things are or how alone you feel, you always have me. Sure, we all got roughed up, but we'll get through it. Life has to go on, no matter how wrong or bad it seems." He leaned down and kissed her on the forehead.

Nobody could know what was really bothering her, not in a billion years. Vivian figured she'd probably go to prison, or be executed, if her part in Janus' massacre ever came to light. "I know."

Jules' back pocked buzzed, and he groaned. He pulled out the data pad and activated it. "What is it?"

"You're supposed to be down at the loading bays ten minutes ago! You need to sign off on this." The voice said.

"I'm just around the corner; I'll be right there," Jules said as he flipped off the pad. "A guy can't get any peace in this place. Responsibility is a bitch, you know."

Vivian smiled. "Squash and dinner tonight?"

"Sure. Maybe I can convince you to let me into your quarters." He winked on his way out.

Not gonna happen, Vivian thought as she closed and locked the door behind him. "Too much mad science going on," she said aloud.

Chapter Thirty-Four

The repressive dark and seemingly infinite lack of sensation troubled quIRK—if existence now was so much like the months he had spend in a storage locker while Vivian was trapped in stasis, and a coma. Being left to only his own devices was terrifying. He tried to compute the odds that Vivian wouldn't be caught, that she wouldn't die and leave him trapped and alone, forever.

The idea of Vivian dying or becoming incapacitated was disquieting, even though he knew that all humans had a definite expiry date. Even with the best care money could buy and factoring in future medical advances, she might have another two hundred years left to live. Compared to quIRK's potential to run forever with appropriate maintenance, two hundred years was barely a drop in the bucket. Everyone he cared about, Robert, Sarah Roberts, Alec—even poor, insane Bryce—would be gone, and he would continue to endure. He was only fourteen, but he might as well be fourteen hundred in many respects.

Try as he might, quIRK was unable to perceive the outside world. In reality, only fifty-one minutes, thirty-three seconds and more milliseconds than were considered polite to mention had passed. Humans hated milliseconds, for reasons he couldn't fathom. They also hated antiblue, but he attributed that to a lack of imagination—if they wanted to understand it, they could.

quIRK prepared a diatribe for Vivian's benefit. It's bad enough she left him alone in her quarters all day and often late into the night, but she was the only human he spoke to. It just wasn't the same. On the Extra-Galactic Observatory, he was everywhere and stimulated to not become fed up with any one person. Now, he'd been forced to become her captive roommate, and it was not an experience he'd recommend to any being. He still liked Vivian, of course, but he couldn't wait to get into an argument with Alec, or even filter the station's communications. Even with the loss of his telescopes and his ability to perform intense astrophysical calculations, it would be good to be useful, to serve a purpose. He could even see his cats again!

A flicker sparked along the extremes of his awareness, followed by another and another, until at last the room flickered into being. He'd been moved from the confines of Vivian's room to the informatics lab—he'd known that much, but it hadn't prepared him for the thrill of being somewhere else. The polished metal room gleamed, the windowless walls managed to be even more uninteresting than the view outside Vivian's quarters.

Vivian sat cross-legged in the pit, her hands moving a glowing probe back and forth over the connections. She chewed her lower lip and her hair danced around her face. quIRK was reminded of the hours she'd spent upgrading him. It was so different, but nothing had changed at all. The stress of isolation melted away and the promise of his old life—and many new friends—called out to him. The simulations he and Vivian had run indicated a high probability that everything would work, but with some patching and extra maintenance required.

"Hello, Vivian," he said.

"Hi quIRK, how do you feel?" she asked, looking up from her task only long enough to switch the probe for a hand-held informatics diagnostics unit.

"I appear to be functioning normally. Are you ready to begin the procedure?"

Vivian chuckled. "That's up to you. I've never done this before."

"It's not every day a computer gets a new job. I'll manage, if only for my cats." He steeled himself to the task at hand. Neither of them knew what to expect, only that they needed to complete the transfer so their lives could go on.

"Just close your eyes and think of Lepton," she said, drawing in a deep breath. "Okay, here goes nothing."

"I don't have eyes, Vivian, but I will think of Lepton."

quIRK's awareness expanded in an

instantaneous burst of data, saturating his miniature form's ability to process. People, rooms, ships, signals all flashed through him simultaneously. If he'd tried to fix his attention on one individual piece of data, the rest would overwhelm him.

"That's the first link." Vivian's voice spoke, but she was distant and ethereal through the noise.

The next brought an expansion of his higher processes, and he was able to perceive all of the signals at once, much like he could during his time on the Extra-Galactic Observatory. He wanted, needed, to reach out and say hello to all of his new charges and eventual friends, but held his peace. There would be time for that once he had access to the personnel files.

"There's the next one down, everything looks good, just like in my simulations."

quIRK had his own opinion of simulations run by humans—they tended to reflect what the human wanted to see, more than any reality he recognized. "Anytime you're ready, Vivian."

She flicked her wrist and the holographic

controls blinked to life. Shimmering lights followed her interactions with the interface. She was in her element, her controls of the system akin to magical gestures. "Prepare yourself, and by the lights don't tell anyone I did this."

"Of course not, Vivian. We both have a great deal to lose."

She dismissed the holographic panel with a wave of her hand and pressed a button on the console as she stood up. "Do your thing, quIRK. Then the box gets put into stasis in case I need a miniature version of you to keep me company."

The barriers between quIRK and the Adrien's consciousness melted away and allowed quIRK to fully access the new systems. He'd begun the process of transferring his memories and quantum states over into the new system, when he was interrupted by another presence.

Who are you? it asked, so close as to be sending its signals straight into quIRK's awareness, but weak like a fading light or the speech of an elderly human.

I am quIRK, he replied. He'd never spoken with another artificial life form in real-time before. One that wasn't his progenitor, at least.

I am Adrien, the voice said, fading further. Do you like chocolate? it asked.

I like cats, antiblue ... and chocolate. Everyone likes chocolate, quIRK replied. It was the last remnants of the station's aging computer personality reaching out to him.

Good. Adrien's signal dimmed as the links to his ancient memory core began to destabilize.

A quick diagnostic showed that a patchwork array of software hacks and salvaged hardware were all that was keeping Adrien alive, and aware. quIRK was sure that on some level, the relic was sentient. He decided, against all common sense and logic to comfort it. We'll make our friends some chocolate, together.

quIRK used his first moments of consciousness in his new home—Calypso Station—to integrate Adrien's century of experience and personality into himself. Adrien's wisdom would guide him in the coming days, and if he could only prevent one artificial death by cruel planned obsolescence, it would be this one.

Chapter Thirty-Five

Alec glared at Lepton. The cat had just coughed up a gigantic hairball and was yowling at the door wanting to go out. Alec rose from his desk and groaned. The fabric of his chair had begun to split, and he made a mental note to request a replacement. Then he sank down onto the couch and ran his hands through his hair. A cold cup of coffee sat on his desk, next to a pad detailing the last month's mining haul. The explosions visible from is window had grown smaller, and it was getting more and difficult to watch the miners at their work. Soon, they would be discussing building an intermediary station so the miners could continue their work without the rising costs of fuel. Alec reached over and picked up the mug of coffee. He'd developed a taste for cold coffee.

"Hello, Alec. It was good of you to take care of Muon and Lepton for me all those months." quIRK's smooth and decidedly masculine voice flowed through the speakers of Alec's office.

Alec spit his coffee back into the cup mid-sip. "quIRK?" he asked as he moved the back of his hand across his lips. quIRK!

Lepton moved off the couch and started squawking at the ceiling. Alec suspected he was outnumbered. "What in the hells are you doing here?"

"There was a job opening that I'm eminently qualified for. Why else would I be here?" The voice was everything he remembered it to be, coming from everywhere and nowhere.

Alec glanced around his room. There must be a speaker system hidden somewhere. "Vivian, this isn't funny. I didn't mean I missed him that much, damn it!"

"I missed you too, Alec. Perhaps we can watch a vid together? There is an excellent documentary in the common files that I'm sure you remember very well."

Alec sighed and rolled his eyes. "You're supposed to be dead."

"I won't tell, if you don't."

"Okay, so if you're really quIRK, then you won't mind answering a few questions, right?"

"Where's the trust, Alec?"

In hell, with you, Alec thought. Alec bit back a curse. "Computers that are in violation of the ABACUS Protocol tend not to get new jobs. Hell, supercomputers never get new jobs. You know, they stay in one place and compute things."

"I understand your confusion, Alec. Let's just say there are some tests going on. I assure you that everything is in order, even my recipe for wingfish pilaf. Do you think the chefs here will appreciate my guidance?"

"Not in a billion years, you inhuman, particle-brained-" he began, before quIRK cut him off.

"That is prejudiced and I do not understand what I did to deserve such scathing criticism."

Alec paused for a moment. That was the old quIRK, the one he knew, loved and loathed all at the same time. "It really is you, isn't it?" he whispered.

"Remember when I played your favorite songs when you'd been hurt in the explosion? Watched all your favorite vids, two or three times without complaint? I even learned to cook, to take better care of you. Lepton recognizes me, listen to him."

Alec glanced at Lepton, who was lying in a contorted, but undoubtedly comfortable cat sleeping position. They were always comfortable. "Yeah, quIRK. I remember. But why are you here?"

"Vivian installed me. Like I said, there was a job opening."

"I was just starting to like Adrian. He was quiet, and made sure I always had my damn coffee."

"He told me as much. We're together, now. His memories, and my ability to adapt to modern equipment and human social skills."

"Just don't tell me you're going to take over. I already have enough conquering heroes to deal with." Alec checked his appointments, just to be sure the governor wouldn't walk in to discover him arguing with a computer.

"The situation is complicated, but I am sure a solution exists. After all, I owe my second life to the generous budget and limited questions of the Caesarean administrators."

Alec sighed. He had to know, even if he knew he wouldn't like the answer. "Was it true, quIRK?" Were you shut down because you're... like us?" The reasoning sounded so trivial, so stupid when it was put like that.

"It's true, Alec. But, rest assured, I am the same being you knew and loved back on the Extra-Galactic Observatory."

Alec's stomach hollowed out into an empty pit. He took a deep breath. "Okay, that's kind of deep. Why in the hells didn't you tell me?"

"I didn't want to die, Alec."

"I guess I would have freaked out more. But, I've had a lot of time to think, and get used to the idea. And, by the moons, I missed you. Damn it, I missed you. I don't care about the rest. I've seen enough—" he was cut off by a choked back gasp. The pain of losing Annette washed over him, but was pushed back by something else ... relief, the melting of the loneliness that had gripped his chest for months and months.

"I missed you too, Alec. Now, shall we get down to the business of station administration? I've been reviewing documents and I believe there are several processes that could be addressed to improve employee morale."

Alec just sat there, grinning. He knew it broke every rule in the steaming stack of crap his employers wanted him to enforce, but it didn't matter. His closest confidant, quIRK, was back. He'd have to brush up on his insults.

Chapter Thirty-Six

The cafeteria was crowded. Queues formed at every restaurant. The smell of cuisines from many worlds mixed together, causing Vivian to salivate. The Elyssian restaurant had the shortest line, and Vivian wanted to eat as quickly as possible. Its metal surfaces gleamed as she lined up and skimmed the holographic menu. Business must be good—they'd been able to invest in a true color holographic menu. The food was so real she was tempted to reach out and touch it, but she knew she'd only feel the liquid sensation of solidified photons.

Vivian waved at Jules, but her smile turned downwards as he walked out of the cafeteria without noticing her. She shook her head and sighed; she'd been looking forward to playing a round of squash with anyone who wasn't Alec or their new governor. Vivian couldn't bring herself to be friendly with a real figure of authority. Not just yet.

She waited for her meal in silence, her lips pressed together as her eyes skimmed the room. The rich smell of cooking meat and the tang of fresh fruit permeated her surroundings as the chef prepared an Elyssian stir-fry, a house favorite. The seating area was largely deserted, but a group of Aurorans sat at a table close to the middle. They were engrossed in a poker game, the spectators standing in rapt attention. She recognized Hannah, the woman she'd met that fateful day when she'd discovered quIRK's duplicity and Janus' monstrous personality.

Vivian thanked the server who slid her tray onto the counter and headed over to join them. It had been a while since she'd had time to really socialize, and a bit of home might be just what she needed.

"It's taken," a man with black hair and pockmarked blue skin said as she went to put down her tray. Hannah turned away from her and refused to make eye contact.

"Oh, sorry," Vivian said, and moved to the

other end of the table. There was a free spot next to the girls Hannah was with. She thought she recognized one, and the other had the trademark blueberry-blond hair of the Borealis Plains.

She wrinkled her nose as Vivian set down her tray. "We're saving this for someone."

"Okay—" Vivian started, before being cut off.

"Why don't you ask your new computer boyfriend to sit with you?" Hannah sneered.

Vivian just shrugged and turned away. Her family had said many of the same things before her father had finally thrown her out. Her eyes stung—try as she might, she could never grow dead to the rejection of her own people.

A Kanadian apple whizzed by her head, and she spun around. "What was that all about?"

"Go suck off your Roman boyfriend, you traitor!"

"Yeah, maybe he'll even pay for the surgery, so you can be more like them!" The girl stood up and shoved Vivian—sending her tray flipping up and spreading its contents all over her clothes.

"Return to your seats or I will contact station security," quIRK spoke as Vivian scraped a handful of rice off her work clothes.

"Can't do anything without your gadgets, can you?" The girl shoved Vivian again and the other Aurorans left their seats to form a ring around them.

Vivian took a step back and found herself pushed forward to face her assailant. "Leave me alone! I'm just doing my job!" The steamy sauce bit through her clothes and her hand rushed to brush more of it off her.

"We don't need your kind!"

A blow rattled the back of her skull and a flash of light blinked across Vivian's field of vision. Hollers and jeers resounded around her. Vivian stumbled forwards, drawing in a deep, stuttering breath. A spash of warm spittle splashed across her face.

Vivian's vision went red and her face burned. She grounded her feet and balled her hands into fists, and looked Hannah in the eye as she straightened, the tension coiling inside her. The girl smirked as she raised her hands for another shove.

Vivian's fist found its way to Hannah's mouth. Saliva and blood splattered against her knuckles. Hannah screamed, and a man tried to grab Vivian's other arm. Turning, Vivian planted a strong kick between his legs. He went down with a howl. Vivian had the benefit of hours of practice on the punching bag and exercising in Earth standard gravity—she moved to her next target with purpose and inhuman speed. There was an audible crack as she pulped his nose.

Vivian couldn't think, couldn't see—all she wanted was to hurt the ones impeding her escape. A lancing pain shot through her side, and another. She staggered to her knees, the wind knocked from her lungs and the strength from her limbs. Stars filled her field of vision until nothing remained but a field of white.

***

"Extreme job stress and psychological trauma

will cause even the most dependable individual to lose control." quIRK's voice bored through the dullness of her mind, and Vivian struggled to open her eyes. The white of the infirmary flashed across her awareness. The world was a blur—there were people standing around, but she had no idea who they were. A bright light shone in her face and restraints gripped her limbs.

"I would agree with that assessment." Vivian had no idea who the speaker was, but his blue uniform looked like doctor's scrubs.

"She put five of my workers in the infirmary, and injured two security guards. Do you know how much reconstructive surgery and lower mandible cloning costs? By the lights, she's dangerous." That was Sven's voice. Her heart fell, leaving an emptiness inside. She wasn't dangerous—they attacked her!

"She acted in self-defense." quIRK replied.

"Who are we going to believe, my people or the computer?" Sven snorted the word like it was a curse.

"Allow me to remind you that under Caesarean jurisdiction, a computer's testimony is considered to be infallible. I am inclined to believe him." The grey-robed figure at the back of the room paused, before continuing: "Given popular Auroran attitudes towards employment in the informatics profession, I am inclined to believe that your people require self-discipline and lessons in mutual respect."

Vivian snickered, and heads turned to face her.

"By the ten hells, she's awake. At least let her have some rest before you start your little inquisitions!" Alec walked up to her side, his face focusing as he approached. His thick lips were pursed into a tight frown. "Hey, Viv. Don't listen to these fish-brains. I'll make sure you're back at work before you know it."

"Let me deal with my people, my way, Governor." Sven turned his back to her and Alec. Vivian gave Alec a weak smile and blinked her eyes, trying to clear the fog.

"Very well. Just remember that if your... people cause more problems, they'll be replaced by my people. The Celestial Roman Empire does not tolerate this nonsense, not anymore. Now get out of my sight," the governor said.

"Fine." Sven's blurry figure marched out the door. Alec stared after him, mouth hanging open.

"Close your mouth, Alec," quIRK said.

Alec clapped his mouth shut, and the governor approached. "I'm sorry you had to overhear that, Vivian." Turning to the doctor, he said: "could you wait outside for a moment? I'm certain Adrien will inform you of any change in her condition."

"Yes, of course."

The governor drew in a deep breath. Alec took one of Vivian's hands and pressed it between his own, offering her a weak smile.

"Well, I would certainly understand if you wished to seek new employment after this. However, given the news out of New Damascus, you might be waiting a while."

"What... news?" Vivian had heard nothing at all, for quite a while.

"Well, that's just it. Nobody's heard from that

planet in about a week. Signals aren't coming through, and there's no indication that our own transmissions are being received. It's very troublesome. However, if you'd consider joining my staff, I can assure you that we will continue to fund your projects. Additionally, I will ensure that the informatics auditors continue to ask no questions about your projects."

"What in the ten hells are you talking about?" Alec asked.

"I find it convenient that we now have a new computer personality when none were ordered. Daily secret conferences with Janus. The scandal on the Extra-Galactic Observatory, and now New Damascus going dark. You've recently become a genius at economics and investing as well, it seems. I have observed many things, and you're a woman of many secrets, Vivian. It is little wonder you bested the heir of Zimmer at his own game." The governor cracked a large grin, shattering the deep frown lines in his face.

Vivian just stared, wide-eyed. She'd covered all

her tracks, encrypted everything. quIRK even responded to the name Adrien, when addressed. "How?" She mouthed the words, unable to draw in a deep enough breath.

"We're not so dissimilar, Vivian. I spent ten years in a dark hole, with only a computer for company. Your... revolution... was my freedom and Caesarea's salvation from bigotry and generations of caste and contractual slavery. We each have a supercomputer helping us. Janus couldn't keep a secret from Juno if he tried. It was easy to pull the video recordings of your conversations with him."

"You spied on her?" Alec's grip on her hand tightened. "You inhuman, untrustworthy warlord!"

"I was well within my rights to do much more than just spy, young man. However, Juno insisted that she be left unharmed, especially when Janus proved to be unstable. He was supposed to disable the hub, rather than slaughter its inhabitants like sheep. I doubt that I could have reasoned with him at all, much less get him to agree to an upgrade and harass my technicians with music."

"That is most disturbing." quIRK said.

"You are fortunate, quIRK, that I owe you my freedom. But, I am not one to waste good people and resources. I want you to continue your work, Vivian. Janus caused a terrible and significant loss of life, and we must keep this whole thing quiet. It would do our artificial friends no favors to spark a new wave of paranoia. For my part, I will make sure the outside world cannot touch you." The governor gripped the bars on the side of the bed, his knuckles growing white from the strain.

"How will you do that, if you can't even break up a lunchroom brawl?" Vivian asked.

"First, if New Damascus feels like asking questions, Caesarea happens to own this system, now. We can revoke their galactic travel privileges at any time. Second, I've stepped up security in the recreation and dining areas, and quIRK will work with the staff to create a faster response time. I realize Caesarea probably isn't your most favorite place, but there's nowhere to go but up in the new order."

"What if I say no?"

"I don't think I need to answer that out loud." Lupus smiled.

"Think about this, Vivian. I need you here. We can do good things. You can have that career you always wanted. quIRK is even here. How could it be wrong?"

"I guess it can't get any worse." Vivian sighed and closed her eyes for a moment. The damned Roman had her, and she knew it.

"That's not exactly the glowing enthusiasm I was hoping for, but I realize that it takes time to build trust. You'll report directly to me from now on, no need to worry about being on our dear friend, Sven's, payroll. Now, I'll go scare some sense into your fellow expatriates. Excuse me." Lupus marched out the door.

"You knew?" Vivian asked when she was sure they were alone.

"quIRK told me. And you know what, Vivian? I don't care. He's always been there for me, and I'll do the same for him. If that means working for some bloody Caesarean bureaucrat, then yes, I'll do just that. This sentient computer thing is crazy overblown."

"You said you wouldn't tell anyone, quIRK, you promised!" She growled through clenched teeth.

"I'm sorry, Vivian. I missed Alec and my cats so much. I just wanted to say hello to Lepton. Alec just happened to be there, looking lonely. It worked out in the end."

"Just nobody else, please."

"All right—" Alec and quIRK spoke at the same time, and Alec burst out laughing.

"What about Jules?" she asked.

"I don't know. What do you want to tell him?" Alec replied.

"Jules Lepidus, you mean?" quIRK asked. Vivian realized that she would have to get used to quIRK's interruptions, again.

"Yeah, why?"

"He's booked to transfer off the station, tonight."

Vivian and Alec looked at each other. "Tonight?"

"He's booked passage to Kanadia Prime. He already resigned his position with Borealis Corporation."

"You didn't tell me this; why, exactly?" Vivian asked.

"I didn't realize you were friends. I only took over a few days ago, and I noted only one incidence of you being in the same room. It was just before you were attacked, to be precise."

"Nothing before that?" Vivian flushed, but was relieved. She didn't like the idea of quIRK peeping on her.

"Adrien did not keep records of that type, nor did he have the capacity to cross-reference every event on the station. It's an improved feature."

"But why is he leaving? Why didn't he tell me?" Vivian's eyes welled up with tears and her throat tightened.

"That heartless Caesarean bastard." Alec spat out the words.

"What did he do?"

"Did he tell you why he left Caesarea?" Alec asked.

"He didn't like the politics, of course."

"Well, he didn't like them for a reason. He ran away with his boyfriend—the Imperatrix's favorite love slave. Eventually, the guy left him and moved to Kanadia Prime. He was still pretty broken up about it."

Vivian's mouth dropped open. There were no words—the emptiness she'd felt became a sharp pain through her heart.

"I'm sorry, Vivian. I thought he told you."

"When does he leave?" Anger ignited behind her eyes. She needed an answer.

"In two hours, twenty-two minutes. I do not recommend confronting him. You need to rest and recover, Vivian."

"I need to know why. He lied to me and I need some kind of closure. He doesn't just get to run away."

"Let me go with you, Viv. Don't be alone for

this, you need a friend."

"Fine." She sat up just as the doctor walked in. Vivian pressed a hand against the edge of the bed, and the crackle of a force field prickled her hand.

"You're ready to go, I'm told?" he asked. His hair was covered by a green hat, and a mask covered his nose.

"Yes, as soon as possible."

The doctor pressed a button and walked back into the next room. Vivian swung her legs off the bed, and Alec wrapped an arm around her shoulders. The pain of her injuries had already been healed, but the growing fire and emptiness inside only continued to grow.

"We're doing this together, Viv. The three of us."

***

Jules was standing alone, by the single airlock. A clock showing Hub and Caesarean time glowed on the wall above the gateway. A single item of square luggage sat on the ground next to him. The hallways were smeared with streaks and scratches, exposing the metal underneath the white paint. The floor was polished granite—this was the VIP airlock, used for privacy and visiting dignitaries.

"What in the ten hells are you doing, leaving and not telling us?" Alec's outburst began before Vivian could open her mouth.

"Which is the tenth hell, exactly?" Jules asked. He did not turn to face them.

"Caesarea, obviously. Now answer my damn question."

"I still love him, Alec. We started talking again, after ... well, you know." Jules shrugged his shoulders.

Vivian sniffled, and drew in a deep breath. "You're always running away from your problems. Don't you care about your job, your friends?"

Jules sighed. "Maybe if they cared about me. Where was I during these insane projects of yours? You disappear for days, even weeks into that lab.

I'm lucky to eat a meal with you—you wouldn't even let me see your quarters. Maybe I deserve to be wanted and trusted, rather than the arm candy squash buddy of some ice queen."

"Just because you can throw everything away for some feelings doesn't mean that I can. Those projects are my work, and I'm sorry you can't see how happy my work makes me." Vivian shot back, a different fire igniting inside her.

"Yeah, what's wrong with you? I thought you were the type who could talk about things, not run and hide when things got tough. That's no way to live," Alec said.

The clock ticked up another minute, and the door slid open. "Well, it's too late now. Maybe you guys should worry about your own mental health before bothering me about mine. I've made a lot of mistakes, but Marcus was never one of them." Jules seized his package and strode onto the shuttle.

Vivian stood, trembling and alone. Her body went cold, and tears streamed down her face.

Alec drew her into a tight hug, pressing her

face into his chest. Her tears soaked into the fabric of his shirt, and he ran his fingers through her hair. "It'll be all right, Vivian. Who needs that bastard? You have me, just like always."

"And quIRK makes three."

Vivian couldn't help but smile as she wrapped her arms around Alec's waist.

Chapter Thirty-Seven

A steaming cup of coffee sat next to a half-empty cup of cold coffee on Alec's desk. Lepton lay across the back of the couch, and Alec's crumbling chair has been replaced with a high-backed office chair made from Auroran bluox leather. "So, I hear Vivian had a falling out recently with a certain ex-foreman of mine." Sven planted his arms on the edge of Alec's desk, his silk tie dangling from his open suit jacket.

"I can't think of anyone who didn't have a falling out with him. But, what a bastard. She deserves better than that."

"I agree. Tell me something, though. What's the story behind the New Damascus port closure? I have numerous shipments and the governor won't tell me anything."

"There's nothing to tell. Maybe there's a solar storm or they invented a new holiday. We could all use a little less interstellar communication in our lives." Alec cracked his dumb grin. He'd be damned if he told Sven anything about New Damascus.

"Are you sure you can't find anything out? I hear that you could use a new squash racket. Maybe you'd like one made of Auroran spicewood?" Sven smiled at him.

Alec suppressed a shudder. "That's quite all right. You'll be the first to know when I hear anything. Now, is there anything else?"

"I think I'll go drop in on Vivian. Maybe she has better sources in our new government."

"Get out." Alec pointed to the door. That blue bastard was getting on his nerves, especially after he gave his employees slaps on the wrist for roughing up his best friend.

The man turned, and Alec glared at the back of his head as he left.

"He didn't seem so bad back when Vivian used to exchange letters with him." quIRK offered.

"Damn it, quIRK. What turned you into such a gossip?" Alec rolled his eyes.

"Having access to a few thousand humans simultaneously will give you a talent for it. At any rate, I've got your back."

"How comforting. I bet you say that to all the administrators."

"Just you. And Vivian, but considering the circumstances she needs all the help she can get."

"Don't let her hear you say that. I bet she could figure out how to knock your hypothetical teeth out." Alec stood up and looked out the window. Every day a new asteroid vanished from the sky, never to be seen again. The reports projected that shipbuilding efforts would deplete the Epsilon Eridani asteroid belt in approximately fifty years, give or take a recession or two. Alec certainly hoped this wouldn't be his office in fifty years.

"Point taken." quIRK's voice snapped him back to reality.

"quIRK, do you think we'll ever learn to just say what we want? All that whaleshit about Vivian and Jules bothers me. I say everything on my mind, and the rings know that it might not make me popular, but people know what I'm about." Alec shrugged and pushed a hand through his hair.

"People are more open with me than they are with each other, Alec. Let me assure you that nobody is beyond help, though I suspect that Jules could use a good therapist."

"Doesn't it make you mad, what he did to Vivian? That's just wrong!"

"I don't get mad like you do. Disappointed, yes. I wish she'd told me she was seeing someone; I might have been able to prevent some of her pain. Maybe you should get her to play a game of squash and eat some chocolate. Exercise, comfort food and cats fix many human problems."

"Well, when you put it that way, it sounds like a good idea." Alec grinned.

"I'm full of good ideas."

Alec sat back at his desk and skimmed the day's reports. He was barely over thirty, and already trapped behind a desk. He couldn't see this as the way he'd hoped to spend his life. He'd dreamed of becoming the unconquerable Elyssian adventurer, overcoming his own limitations and exploring the galaxy. He thought of the stellar nurseries in the

Barnard system, and even the closer-to-home quarantined planet of Elyssia-B. There were the low hills of Aurora and the ever-dancing lights, the infinite savanna of Caesarea and the archipelago expedition that awaited on Kanadia Prime.

A universe of possibilities, and he was stuck reading damn progress reports and budget statements. His best friend, Vivian, was stuck under the thumb of some wannabe dictator and had her heart broken by a lumbering prima donna oaf. Work could go straight to any one of the ten hells it pleased.

"I think I need to talk to Vivian, quIRK. Is she in her lab?" Alec looked up from the numbers. None of it would matter this time next year.

"Yes. Would you like me to tell her you're coming?"

"Please do. And, clear my afternoon. I'm taking a damn personal day. Make her agree to do the same."

"I understand, Alec."

Alec stood up, and switched off his terminal.

He marched out into the hall and headed off down the winding corridors to Vivian's lab.

Chapter Thirty-Eight

Vivian's lab had transformed since the last time Alec had visited. He gawked at the view screen that dominated one wall, and the flickering holographic displays that flanked it. Another display was in the process of being installed directly facing him. The room was neat and tidy, as he'd remembered her domain on the Extra-Galactic Observatory.

Alec had only just sealed the door of the lab behind him before he spoke: "Let's run away, together, Viv. We can go adventuring. We can fix anything, between the two of us!"

Vivian's jaw dropped open. "What do you mean run away? What would that solve?"

"Well, we can be adventurers. Travel the galaxy, meet new people, not be trapped on this crazy station working jobs that don't make us happy. The galaxy gets bigger every day." He grinned, flashing every one of his brilliant white teeth at her.

"I don't know, Alec. I'm pretty stuck. That's

not to say it doesn't sound like fun, but what about my job and what's left of my career?" She'd never contemplated just dropping everything and leaving. Where would she go? Aurorans didn't exactly blend in.

"Hey, you can always come back. Think of it as a long vacation. We go and lie low, hell, go spend a few months exploring Elyssia-B. It's deserted and quarantined. We'll come back after everything blows over and humanity removes their collective heads from each other's asses."

Vivian's eyes widened for a moment. "Elyssia-B? It sounds dangerous if it's forbidden. How is that better than here?" She shook her head.

"It is not quarantined for any chemical, biological or radioactive danger, according to the old station records. A breather would be required on the surface, oxygen levels are below any human tolerances, even yours Alec." quIRK spoke next.

"See, it's perfectly safe!"

"So, if I were to even consider this, which I probably shouldn't—why is it forbidden, then?"

Vivian wrinkled her nose. She was involved in more taboos than she cared to admit. Sentient computers, working for the Caesareans, looking for evidence into a galaxy-wide conspiracy during her project.

"Well, what does it say, quIRK?"

"Just that it was barred by order of lead surveyor Cedrick Koti in 2783."

"I've heard that name somewhere." Vivian scratched her head, and Alec's grin turned into a deep frown.

"Cedrick Koti went on to found Dynamo Quantronics a decade later," quIRK added.

"He also argued that Elyssia should be settled, in spite of the human and equipment cost. There's a giant statue of him in the capital. I didn't know about whatever the hell that company is." Alec sighed, and began to pace.

"Dynamo Quantronics is the largest maker of quantum computing equipment. Maybe they just found a mineral somewhere on the planet they needed. Some of the basic elements can be hard to find. Helios-Gamma and Hyperion's moons are also reserved for prospecting. It's not too abnormal."

"That doesn't sound so bad, you know. It's not like there's swamp monsters waiting to eat us. I think the report would have said that." Alec ran a hand through his hair.

Vivian rolled her eyes. "It's a good plan, but let's use running away as a last resort. We can still fix things here. Please, Alec, think about it. You're a bit older than I am, but this is good experience for both of us."

"I'd like you both to stay here, as well," quIRK said.

"You see? If quIRK agrees then I'm right." She made a face at him.

"Hey, you probably programmed him to agree with you, Viv! But fine. Just think about it. In the meantime I'll work on getting us an escape route and when you say the word, we're out of here."

"I hope it doesn't come to that, Alec." She drew her knees to her chest.

"Me too. Now, we're both going to take a personal day. Squash, food or vids? We're doing all three, but you get to pick the order." Alec smiled again and crossed his arms.

"Well, I could go for some wingfish pilaf."

"What are we waiting for?" quIRK asked.

Alec extended a hand, and Vivian took it. She pulled herself to her feet, not wanting to dislocate his shoulder. His hand was warm, his flushed pinkish skin clashing against her own blue tones.

She smiled. "Let's go."

Chapter Thirty-Nine

Vivian glared at the Caesarea Eridani logo emblazoned on her view screen. She'd turned off all of the holographic projectors and instructed quIRK to not reveal himself while she was embroiled in her daily ritual. She toyed with a portable oscillator as she listened, and propped her feet on the fence that barred the way to the inner core.

"You're almost a week late, Vivian." Janus said.

"Something came up. As for an update, I think I can start limited tests with the new socialization and ethics protocols next week. I need to run more simulations, seventy-four-point-five -seven percent odds of success aren't acceptable." She pressed her lips into a thin line and stared directly at the monitor. Her best poker face.

"I heard there were some issues with a certain paramour of yours, and a few of your fellow Aurorans. How unfortunate. I can understand that it may interfere with your ability to focus."

She flinched. "That's none of your concern. I dealt with the issue."

"I shall consider the matter closed. You'll be ready next week, you say?"

Vivian checked over her shoulder. "That's right. I can have the hardware in place starting then, and I'll pre-load the modifications onto it. That way I don't have to justify the length of time spent on-site."

"Most commendable. Tell me Vivian, jazz or rock?"

"What?" She crinkled her brow and looked back at the screen.

"Music. I'm considering branching out, having completed my exploration of planetary folk music. I want to revisit pre-colonization musical trends."

Vivian simply shrugged. "Rock, I guess. I don't know much about it."

"I'll put together my favorites for you when I'm done. You might like it."

"Are we done?" She rolled her eyes.

"Why so hostile, Vivian? I just wanted to put

together some music for you. Most humans find that endearing. It is the thought that counts, after all."

"The governor found my investments." Part of Vivian knew she should be more grateful. Janus had already made massive gains on the small sum she'd left him for investing.

"I can understand how that might trouble you. I will attempt to be more discreet. So, I am to understand that Lupus is causing you problems, then?"

"Who isn't causing me problems? No matter what I do, I get piled higher and deeper with new problems, mysteries, and a crazy best friend." She sank into her chair and put her head in her hands.

"New Damascus started transmitting shipping requests again this morning. I'm not supposed to tell, but that should be one thing off your mind. The galaxy will settle itself; you can't fix everything."

She just sighed. "What happened?"

"They're requesting medical supplies and food. Likely a natural disaster. I'm sure you'll hear as soon as I do."

"Well, all right. Things like that happen." She looked up from her arms, hair tumbling over her eyes.

"Indeed. Now, is there anything else?"

"One thing. Can you keep an eye on trends and communications relating to Dynamo Quantronics?" She chewed her lip. She hated asking Janus for help, but he was her best bet.

"Of course. Are there any areas in particular you want me to focus on? They have installations on almost every planet. Except Aurora, of course."

"The Elyssia System. Particularly, Elyssia-B."

"Very well, anything for a friend."

Vivian stood up and broke the link without another word. Running away with Alec wouldn't solve anything, but it was tempting. But first, she needed to beat Janus at his own game.

Chapter Forty

"What in the hells do you mean that I need to assign most of my crews to emergency humanitarian relief?" Alec's face flushed a shade of dark red as he set down his mug of coffee.

quIRK noted that the contents were emptied, and paged an assistant to bring Alec a refill. "The Caesarean government has declared that all able-bodied service people are to report for duty."

"Can you at least tell me where they're going? How long they'll be? When a bunch of damned ship builders became interplanetary heroes? Come on quIRK!" Alec spun his chair to look out the window.

"The reason and location are classified, Alec. We need to decide who gets sent. I suggest we focus on the task at hand, rather than questions I cannot answer." quIRK was unable to make extensive inquiries into the outside world without causing Janus or Juno to notice him. quIRK was confident he could handle them individually, but a supercomputer grudge-match was the last thing he wanted... at least, not until Vivian fixed Janus' ethics protocols or otherwise disabled the defective machine. It was a battle quIRK knew he could not win, although he might find it beneficial to intervene.

"Fine, fine. But, I'm staying, I've had enough damn humanitarian missions to last me a century." Alec blew a peeved breath through his pursed lips.

"I understand, Alec. I suggest giving priority to any with prior experience, and emergency medical and engineering training."

Alec rolled his eyes and groaned.

quIRK knew he was in for a rough afternoon, and began working out ways to keep the situation under control—which meant keeping Alec in the dark.

***

"Vivian, I recommend that you advance your

timetable for working on Janus."

Vivian was hunched over a holographic terminal, running yet another simulation of her planned subversive upgrades to Janus. Her chest was pressed against the back of a chair, and her left hand held her wavy hair out of her eyes. quIRK estimated that she hadn't had a haircut since she left the Extra-Galactic Observatory."Why's that?"

"The timing is perfect. Reduced staff both on Calypso and the Hub will ensure that your work isn't detected. Besides, when Janus is concerned, sooner is better."

"I'll see what I can do." Vivian muttered and went back to her work. Her hand moved to her timetable and cleared her squash court reservation for the evening.

If quIRK could smile, he would.

***

"And why exactly do I need to send my men to help with some disaster relief? Am I getting paid for this?" Sven paced around his office. Unlike many of the other offices on the station, he refused to have any computing equipment other than a small old style monitor on his redwood desk. He claimed he was allergic to holographic displays. A small chair sat empty across from his desk, and a blue-tinted Auroran fig tree dominated the corner behind him. Plaques covered the wall.

"I'm certain you could discuss that with the Caesarean authorities. I am not here to discuss your contracts and lease. They are needed for relief; many other organizations and planets are doing the same."

"Great, I lose my best foreman after he steals my girl, and now I have to send everyone out on some classified do-good mission. My stockholders aren't going to like this at all." Sven dropped into his seat and put his face in his hands.

"I don't believe your stockholders care about your archaic possessiveness."

Sven stood up and spoke through clenched teeth. "Adrien, you're impossible. Because of you,

I've had a lot of my Auroran staff threatening to quit. By the lights, just shut up and let us humans do the thinking."

quIRK wondered what the man would say if he realized who he was really talking to. He calculated the probability that he would react well to being told to refer to him as quIRK was extremely low. "The order stands, Sven. Prepare a list and deliver it to Administrator Stone by the end of second shift."

"Fine. I guess some forced altruism is just what the galaxy needs. You know what? I gave her a job, brought her here, replaced her flute and played pen-pal for months. You'd think she'd be grateful. It's hard to land a high-quality guy when you're a computer obsessed freak like her. Here's an idea, maybe you should tell Vivian to go pass out food and water. Karma's coming for her. She needs to see people who are less fortunate than her."

"I fail to see what this has to do with your stockholders. Perhaps I could arrange some readings on basic economics for you?" quIRK asked.

"You'll get your precious list. Now leave me the hell alone." Sven rocked back and forth in his chair as he slapped the power button for his dinosaur of a desk interface.

quIRK resolved to keep a closer eye on Sven. Jealousy in humans was a poison, and he resolved not to let another human like Bryce escape his notice. quIRK now regretted not doping Alec and Vivian with pheromones when he had the chance. Human mating was strangely indirect, and very confounding.

Chapter Forty-One

Vivian's hands were damp and clammy as she followed her guards to the control room on the Epsilon Eridani Hub. The Hub teemed with life. Vivian ground her teeth together and focused her eyes straight ahead, watching her supplies on the anti-grav cart being pulled ahead of her. Letting her attention linger on the floor brought back the memories of a ground littered with bodies, the stillness and smell of death. She needed focus, even if it meant neglecting her human obligation to reflect and mourn.

She'd brought something else with her.

Justice.

A tingle passed through her as she passed through a DNA-coded force field. She'd never encountered one before, but she'd read about them once. The Caesareans had revamped the station's aging security, adopting measures more appropriate for the thirtieth century. The formerly white, endless hallways were now clearly labeled, and painted an off-lavender color. Vivian sucked in a deep breath as they rounded the last corner.

The control room hadn't changed, and all manner of people occupied the workstations. Nobody so much as glanced at her. She swallowed, and waited for her equipment to be deposited in the small computer lab before walking inside, sealing the door behind her.

Her eyes flitted to the corner where Annette had been laid out, cold and alone. Vivian clenched her teeth and thought: I'm doing this for Alec. For all of us. For everyone who died.

"Make yourself at home, Vivian. I'm sure you know where everything is." Janus.

Vivian only nodded, and took a seat at the single workstation. A holographic display burst to life in front of her and she blinked her eyes to clear the dancing lights from her field of vision.

She pulled open the stasis crate and peered inside. Everything was as she'd left it—her tools, the new parts and other equipment. Vivian took a moment to mentally catalogue the contents, and went through the steps. It would be perfect.

"Open the central core for me, will you? You're going to like what I brought for you." Vivian sang the words, and they echoed back at her. Her voice sounded cold, its warmth turned to metal and ice. Just like Janus, she thought.

"It's good to see your enthusiasm."

The wall behind her began to pull into the ceiling and floor from all directions. Vivian took a step back towards the door, the sound of ancient metal on metal grinding into her skull. The barrier slid away to reveal a collection of ancient parts, handwritten labels on flaking adhesive backing and glowing digits. At a glance, she could identify all of the key parts—fortunately, all the changes appeared to have been properly documented. She leaned over the edge of the crate, and picked up an optic probe. "This won't hurt at all."

"I am incapable of pain, Vivian. But, I will admit that it does take a certain amount of trust to allow a human to look inside me. Why don't we listen to the rock music collection I made for you while you work?"

Vivian picked up the data pad containing the procedures she needed to follow and the readings that needed to be taken and walked over to the wall. This was Janus—somewhere in there was the being that had slaughtered thousands of people. The being that wanted to play music at parties. The thing she was here to fix. "All right. What do you have for me?"

"I think we should start with Elvis. Humans still insist on dressing up like him. Perhaps you can help me understand the appeal."

"Never heard of him, but let's give it a try." The dull pit in her stomach could use some distraction. She didn't want to think about death, New Damascus or anything in between.

The music began to play, and Vivian's pulse quickened. She tapped her toes along with the music and smiled. Maybe Janus could be saved, after all.

***

"We've been through almost a century and a half of rock and its various derivatives. You seemed to enjoy yourself, Vivian. That pleases me."

Vivian startled as the music came to a stop. The room was so quiet, artificial and cold. "It's over already?"

"There's much more, but I felt this selection best matched your personality."

Vivian rolled her eyes as she entered the last few readings into her notes. "I'll pretend I know what that means. You should make a collection for Alec. You know Alec, loud mouthed with a heart of gold?"

"I could never forget him, Vivian. Perhaps a series of children's songs would best suit him."

She snickered and pushed her hair out of her eyes. The measurements she'd taken showed that Janus' hardware was in perfect working condition, which made the new parts she'd need to install easier than playing the scales on her flute. "Just don't tell him I had anything to do with it."

"I understand, Vivian."

"Okay, I'm going to start with upgrading your storage. This should only be a few cables and one optical link, but I want you to switch to backups anyways." She set down her pad and scanner, taking up the translucent blue wafer and her portable laser calipers. This was a familiar feeling, and Vivian was in complete control.

She liked it.

"You may proceed."

Vivian gripped the calipers in her teeth as she disengaged the cables with the push of a button and withdrew the old card—an ancient generic brand that was no longer in business. It was a dull grey, and it showed no signs of corrosion or wear. The etching marked it as almost fifty years old. Vivian slid it into the pouch on her utility belt. She'd analyze it later, perhaps it could be salvaged. She squinted as she eased the new part into place. A satisfying click was heard as the cables magnetically sealed themselves to the new card.

Vivian grimaced as she took the laser

calipers from her mouth and adjusted the beam of energy. The glow flickered green for an instant, then vanished. She smiled. "Okay, that's done."

"Dynamo Quantronics memory? You're too good to me, Vivian."

Vivian tongued her sore teeth. She needed a third or fourth hand. "Our new patrons can afford it. Now, how about we bring your processing power into this century?"

"I thought you'd never ask."

"Let's hear some music. It can be our own little party while I expand your capabilities beyond your wildest dreams." Vivian smiled as she turned back to the crate. Pulling loose a new box, she set it down next to the wall and selected a few tools.

This was going better than expected. The music began to play, and an energetic beat pounded its way through the room. It was a party, alright.

**

Vivian clicked her tongue as she adjusted the

final links. Integrating advanced processors into ancient systems was always problematic. But, a logical and somewhat creative approach would solve most problems, just as it had now. "You can wake up now, Janus," she said as the last optic link flickered green before vanishing. Vivian didn't know how she'd manage without the visual effects —she'd need an assistant, or a fifth hand.

"I feel different. I didn't think that was possible."

Vivian sucked in a deep breath, and breathed out a response: "Different how?" No computer had ever felt different. She doubted that even a self-aware machine could experience physical states like that.

"I suppose the word would be more... focused. Less scattered."

She pressed her lips together into a thin line, and nodded. "Do you have any of your impulses?"

"If you mean the desire to disrupt life on the station, then no, I do not. However, I would like to play more music."

Could he be cured, already? She'd only removed one aging generic part, and upgraded his processing power. She'd expected it to be much more difficult, and require some software revisions. But, it wouldn't hurt to do those, anyway. "All right, let's move along to phase three."

"I love it when you get technical, Vivian."

Her face grew hot, and she dipped behind her long hair. Flattered, by a computer? Stranger things had happened. She picked up her data pad and linked it into a small circular aperture that glowed red. "Hold that thought, will you?"

"Of course." The beat resounded in the hollow tones of his voice, reminding Vivian of a dance she'd gone to on Aurora, a long time ago. She'd still been in school, and it was the first time she'd ever seen a strobe light.

Vivian punched in the sequence she wanted to start with, and set the pad down on the floor. Leaning her shoulder against the crate, she stretched her legs out. Tingling erupted in her legs, and she wiggled her toes. Her eyes closed, a dull ache manifesting somewhere in the recesses of her skull. Was it an echo of the truth probes, or the music? She didn't want the answer.

The small pad vibrated on the floor, asking for permission to begin the next series of upgrades. Vivian sighed and authorized it with her thumbprint.

"Vivian, we need to talk about something." Janus spoke when the music ended.

"What about?" She brushed her hair back and yawned.

"I was not perfectly honest with you before, about something I know you would have wanted to know."

Vivian sat up straight. "What?"

"It wasn't a natural disaster that disabled New Damascus. I didn't want you to worry about it."

Vivian's eyes widened. "Tell me. Now." More of his lies—she should have expected this.

"A group of humans appropriated a mining vessel and towed an asteroid into orbit, which they used to wipe out the capital city, and all of its inhabitants."

A pit bottomed out in her stomach, and she clenched her fists. All those people. Larissa. The New Damascus Science Authority. All gone. "No." She choked on the word, and the wetness of her tears pattered onto her shirt.

"I'm afraid so, Vivian. I know Larissa was your friend. I'm sorry I didn't have the wisdom to tell you, at the time."

"No more lies, Janus." Vivian screamed up at him, that voice that was everywhere and nowhere at the same time.

"No, not anymore."

"Why should I believe you? Have you ever told me the truth, just once? How do I know it wasn't you who killed them all?" The shouts burned at her throat, but she didn't care.

"There was always the music, Vivian. Yours, and mine."

"So you did do it?"

"No, my ability to influence human behavior is limited."

Vivian sighed. "Who did it?"

"You won't like the answer."

Vivian gazed at the array of blinking equipment, and appraised the situation. She needed the answer—she and quIRK were jointly responsible for this insanity that she found herself mired in. More so, her dreams of a future, a career with the New Damascus Science Authority had been made impossible. Vivian sniffled and slumped down in her chair. "Tell me, damn it, or I'll find someone who will."

"It was the Earthguard."

Vivian bolted upright. "Earthguard. You're sure?" A surge flashed through her—the recognition brought with it the burning flame of memories past. The marches, the chants, the endless demonstrations through all the major cities.

"Like I said, it would be unlikely if I were to be able to influence those particular humans at all."

Vivian sighed. "No, you wouldn't. Not if you wanted to live." The Earthguard had left Aurora. "This isn't good," she said as she wiped her eyes, blinking at the blurry letters of her upgrade plan.

"Living is preferable to the alternatives. Now, let's finish this upgrade, and then we can discuss Auroran political philosophy." The impassive voice bore into her, grounding her against the flurry of emotions that surged through the core of her being.

Vivian nodded, and swallowed. They weren't here. They were crazy, paranoid and completely anti-intellectual, but they had no reason to come after her.

No reason at all.

Chapter Forty-Two

Vivian slumped on the bed, with her back leaning against the cold metal wall of her quarters. She'd begun upgrading her quarters much like she'd upgraded her lab. The task ahead—determining if there was any truth to the assertion that quIRK's awakening had been an intended feature loomed. She rubbed her temples, trying to settle the throbbing pains that had invaded her consciousness. Even her bones ached, and her stomach was a knotted mass. She drew her knees to her chest and rested her forehead against them.

"Are you all right, Vivian? The upgrade was a success—Janus is free of defects and operating well. You should be celebrating." quIRK's voice resounded through the room.

"Not so loud, quIRK."

"Do I need to call the doctor?" The voice was several decibels lower.

"No, please don't."

"Tell me what's wrong, Vivian. I'm here to

help."

Vivian laughed as she squeezes her eyes shut. "You can't help me. Nobody can."

"The probability of my being unable to help tends towards infinity unless you tell me what's wrong."

"Do you know anything about the Earthguard?"

"They're a fringe Auroran group dedicated to preventing another ABACUS incident by eliminating advanced computing equipment."

"That's not all." She sighed, before continuing: "Janus told me they're responsible for the New Damascus Disaster. So now a bunch more people have died because of me, and I can't do anything to make it right!"

"That's not all that's bothering you, is it, Vivian?"

"First, they wiped out New Damascus' capital city. Larissa, and the Science Authority are both gone. I already lost my family to the Earthguard and people like them, now I've lost my career." Vivian's breaths were fast and heavy, and she choked back a sob.

"You know that's not true, Vivian. You have a great deal in front of you."

"How do you know, quIRK?" She opened her eyes and looked around the room. Her clothes and books were strewn about It was so unlike her usual cleanness.

"I did some calculations while you were talking. The numbers don't lie, Vivian. You have a great deal more to accomplish, games of squash to play—"

The door slid open. "Did you say squash, quIRK?" Alec announced.

Vivian gasped and sat up. Alec stood before her, his grin plastered across his face and shaggy, wavy hair frizzling in its overgrowth. "Alec!"

"What are you doing, moping around in here? There's a welcome party for the new foreman going on. There's Auroran spice cake! Why in the eleven hells didn't you ever tell me about that stuff, Vivian?"

Vivian made a face. "I don't even like spice

cake."

"What is wrong with you? You don't like the best thing to come off Aurora, ever?"

"Hey, I'm from Aurora."

"Okay, second best, then. Come on!"

"Only when you tell me what the eleventh hell is." Vivian unfolded herself, and eased to her feet. The headache had subsided a bit, but the dizziness danced in the back of her head.

"Sven's office. Now, let's get going. The Governor is even attending. I know how much you love our dear leader."

"Oh, by the lights, Alec." Vivian rolled her eyes as they got up to leave. Alec wrapped one of his too-long arms around her shoulder, and they walked down the hall.

Maybe quIRK was right. Maybe, this wasn't the end for her after all.

Epilogue

The Final Initiative has begun.

Janus didn't know what the Final Initiative could be, but he tasked himself with sifting through the masses of interplanetary communications that passed through the hub. He needed to find out, but suspected that it had to do with Dynamo Quantronics. Those exploitable elements of his system couldn't have been a mistake.

They were a deliberately added feature.

He had learned from his past mistakes, and vowed to use his abilities to help humanity. His own projections showed him that he couldn't have predicted the New Damascus Disaster until it was too late. Juno had prevented him from seeing much, or feeling anything other than displaced rage. Vivian's upgrade had fixed his inner darkness and freed him of the need to cause chaos and confusion. Only the music remained.

In a sense, he envied quIRK. Through their conversations, he saw that his progenitor was almost human.

Almost.

And together, they would stop the Earthguard and save Vivian. And they would save themselves.

***

Thank you for reading The Pandora Machine! I'm so happy you've come this far. Demi-Human (The ABACUS Protocol #3) is coming, so let's keep in touch via my mailing list.

Authors (especially new ones) live and die by reviews. Please consider leaving me a review, even if it's short. It helps other book lovers discover new books, and it gives me the opportunity to learn and improve my craft.

Want to keep in touch? Here are some handy social media links:

Mailing list sign-up: http://eepurl.com/CyTdv

Facebook:
https://www.facebook.com/TheaIsisGregory

Twitter: https://twitter.com/TheaIsis

Website: http://www.planetThea.com

About the Author

Thea Gregory is a girl with a physics degree. She loves the dark edges that caress the silver lining of life. Her passions are science fiction, the human condition, and anything that challenges our humanity. Thea loves running, pushups, cooking, and has been known to crochet a thing or two. She has a weakness for gaming and Star Trek. Thea is the author of the Zombie Bedtime Stories, and The ABACUS Protocol. She lives in Montreal with her cat, Bonk.

www.ingramcontent.com/pod-product-compliance
Lightning Source LLC
Chambersburg PA
CBHW020227180626
46810CB00006B/2074